MAKING THE TEAM
Kelsey Blair

James Lorimer & Company Ltd., Publishers
Toronto

James Lorimer & Company Ltd., Publishers acknowledges the support of the Ontario Arts Council (OAC), an agency of the Government of Ontario, which in 2015-16 funded 1,676 individual artists and 1,125 organizations in 209 communities across Ontario for a total of $50.5 million. We acknowledge the support of the Canada Council for the Arts, which last year invested $153 million to bring the arts to Canadians throughout the country. This project has been made possible in part by the Government of Canada and with the support of the Ontario Media Development Corporation.

978-1-4594-1140-1
eBook also available 978-1-4594-1138-8

Cataloguing data available from Library and Archives Canada.

Published by:
James Lorimer &
Company Ltd., Publishers
117 Peter Street,
Suite 304
Toronto, ON, Canada
M5V 0M3
www.lorimer.ca

Distributed by:
Lerner Publishing Services
1251 Washington Ave N
Minneapolis, MN, USA
55401
www.lernerbooks.com

Printed and bound in Canada.
Manufactured by Friesens Corporation in Altona, Manitoba, Canada in December 2016.
Job #228982

With thanks to Jocelyn and Taylor for coming with me on this and all the other journeys.

For Mom and Dad.

CONTENTS

1 TRYOUTS

Hannah Williams stands on the basketball court at Central Vancouver Middle School. Around her, players warm up for the final day of grade eight basketball tryouts. Balls bounce against the hardwood floor. Hannah spins the basketball in her hands. The bumpy texture of the ball feels good against her palms. The orange of the ball stands out against her dark skin. Hannah waits until the ball is finished spinning. Then she bends her elbow, turns her feet toward a hoop, and shoots. The ball clanks off the rim.

"Nice-looking shot," says June Kan, Hannah's best friend.

"I missed."

"But it looked good. That's what counts." June grabs Hannah's basketball and passes it back to her. Hannah bends her elbow and takes another shot. This time, the ball easily falls through the mesh of the hoop. "Nice."

The coach, Mr. Suto, blows his whistle. All the players jog to centre court to meet him.

"Welcome to the last day of tryouts," he says. His voice booms and Hannah's heart pounds. "At the end of today, I'll announce the team. But no decisions have been made yet. I expect everyone to keep working as hard as they did in the first two tryouts. Understand?" The players nod. "Three lines on the baseline. Balls in the middle line. The player in the middle line passes to the player in the line on her left. The player in the right line sprints down the court. The player from the left line passes to the player in the right line, who does a layup. When you come back, change lines."

Hannah is first in line in the middle line.

"Go!" shouts Mr. Suto.

Hannah passes the ball to the player on her left, Taylor Brown. The pass is a little high, but Taylor is tall and strong. She easily catches the ball and passes to Malaya, the player in the right line. Malaya catches the ball. She completes right-handed layup footwork, stepping forward with her left foot, then her right foot, and finally planting her left foot and jumping. As she pushes off her left foot, she holds the basketball with her right hand and extends it into the air. She shoots the ball with her right hand. It's the perfect layup, and she scores.

"Good work," says Mr. Suto.

Hannah jogs back and switches lines so that she is on the right side of the court. Taylor and Malaya have also switched lines. Taylor lines up in the middle. When she gets to the front of the line, Taylor passes the ball to Malaya, who is on her left. Hannah sprints down the court. As she nears the three-point line, she sees that she will have to do her layup right-handed. Malaya looks at Hannah.

Hannah scrambles to get her foot down in time. She stumbles and ends up jumping off the wrong foot. She shoots with her left hand instead of her right.

"Hannah, I know you're left-handed," says Mr. Suto. "But you've got to learn to use your right hand for right-handed layups."

"Sorry," mumbles Hannah.

"Don't be sorry," says Mr. Suto with a smile. "Just correct it next time."

Hannah jogs to the back of the line. She waits for the chance to try again.

June lines up behind Hannah. She leans in to Hannah's ear. "This drill is boring."

Mr. Suto blows his whistle. "We're going to add something to the drill —"

"Good," whispers June.

Hannah struggles to focus with June talking to her.

Mr. Suto finishes his instructions: "— player becomes the defence. Then the other two players will play two-on-one. Next group up. Let's go."

Hannah turns to June. "Which player becomes defence?"

"Uh … the middle line?"

"Okay."

Taylor, who is in the middle line, passes the ball to the player in the line on her left. Hannah runs down the right side of the court. She is going to get the ball in a position to do the layup again. Hannah snatches the ball out of mid-air.

Mr. Suto told me to shoot with my right hand.

Hannah awkwardly shoots the ball with her right hand. It bounces off the backboard, clanks onto the rim, and falls through the hoop.

"Nice shot, Hannah," cheers June.

Hannah feels a surge of pride pulse through her body.

"Hannah, you're supposed to be on defence now," yells another player from the baseline.

"What?"

Hannah turns her head. Taylor is already charging toward the opposite basket. Hannah runs after her, but it's no use. Hannah barely makes it to the three-point line before Taylor scores.

Mr. Suto blows the whistle. "Remember, the player that does the layup is on defence." Hannah lets out a long sigh. As the drill continues, Hannah gets more chances to score layups and play defence. But she can't shake the gnarly feeling in her stomach.

I should've been listening.

During a water break midway through the tryout, June bounces up to Hannah. "You did really well in that last shooting drill."

"Thanks," replies Hannah. "You too."

"I wonder if we get to choose our uniform numbers this year."

"I don't know."

"I want to be number 10. I wonder what colour they'll be."

"Blue and yellow?" Hannah shrugs. "Those are our school colours."

"I can't wait for the high school team next year. The purple uniforms look so good."

Hannah remembers when June thought their middle school uniforms were the best. Before basketball tryouts in grade seven, they were eating lunch and June was sharing her mom's homemade cookies. Hannah wasn't sure she wanted to play basketball. As June gave Hannah a cookie, she looked her right in the eye. June said, "You've got to try out. The uniforms are so pretty!"

Hannah looks at June and smiles.

I'm so glad June encouraged me to try out. Playing basketball was the best decision I made last year.

Mr. Suto blows the whistle.

"The tryout is almost finished. You've all worked very hard. But we can only have twelve players on the roster this year. I'm going to talk to each of you one-on-one. Shoot free throws until I call you over. Once I've talked to you, you're free to go."

Before Hannah has time to think, June grabs her wrist. "Hannah and I call this hoop," says June to the others. She drags Hannah toward one of the main hoops. "Hannah, you can shoot first."

June passes Hannah the ball. Hannah lines up at the free-throw line. She glances to the corner of the gym, where Mr. Suto stands.

"June Kan!" yells Mr. Suto.

Hannah watches as June jogs to where Mr. Suto is standing. June looks calm and confident as she stops in front of Mr. Suto. A few moments later, she's grinning from ear to ear.

She must've made the team!

Hannah clenches the ball in her hand.

"Hannah Williams!" calls out Mr. Suto.

Hannah drops the ball and sprints toward him.

"Hannah," begins Mr. Suto, "I think you worked hard throughout the tryout, and I was very impressed by your left-handed layups."

"Thanks!"

"As you know, this is a very talented group of players." Mr. Suto's gaze shifts to the corner of the gym and then back to Hannah. He exhales loudly. "I'm sorry, Hannah. You didn't make the team this year."

2 THE LONG WALK HOME

Hannah feels all the air rush out of her body. Mr. Suto's expression is firm, but there's something in his eye.

Is that pity?

Hannah looks away quickly. To her right, there's a door.

I could leave right now.

She takes a step toward it.

My coat ... and my bag.

"Hannah," says Mr. Suto, "if you have any questions about the tryouts or why you didn't make the team, I'd be happy to answer them."

"Nope," says Hannah quickly. She can feel the tears welling behind her eyes,

Don't cry. Don't. Cry.

Hannah puts her head down and charges off toward her backpack.

"I made the team!" announces June.

"I didn't."

"Oh."

Hannah waits for June to do something. Maybe June will be mad at Mr. Suto. Maybe she'll go yell at him.

"That sucks," is all June says.

In the corner, Mr. Suto is talking to Taylor. Both of them are smiling. Hannah looks around the gym. She doesn't want to face all the players who made the team.

I wish Mom wasn't at work. Then she'd be here to drive me home.

"I'm going to walk home."

"I'll come with you," says June quickly.

Hannah throws on her coat and rushes out of the gym. The moment she gets outside, she's hit by chilly January air. Hannah replays every moment from the three tryouts in her head. She was good in the shooting drills. And she scored all her left-handed layups. Right-handed layups? Not as good. And she messed up the two-on-one drill earlier. Did a couple little mistakes really cost her a spot on the team? Were all the other players really that much better than her?

Maybe Mr. Suto doesn't like me?

"It sucks you didn't make the team," says June, running to catch up.

"Yeah."

"You'll just have to make next year's team."

Hannah's heart sinks.

If I couldn't make the middle school team, how am I going to make the high school team?

"You can come watch all our games this year," says June excitedly. "That'll be fun. I'll make sure you're invited to all the team parties."

"Thanks," says Hannah, but she knows it won't be the same as being on the team with June.

They stop at June's corner. "I'll see you tomorrow," June says, and pulls Hannah into a big hug. Hannah feels the tears in her eyes start to well up again.

"See you tomorrow," says Hannah, pulling away quickly.

Hannah watches June walk down her driveway toward the large two-storey house. When June closes the front door behind her, Hannah lets herself cry.

I don't get to play basketball this year.

Hannah uses the sleeve of her hoodie to wipe the tears away. More droplets gather in her eyes. Hannah looks around. If she's going to cry, she'd rather do it at home. Hannah starts to walk the three blocks from June's street to her house. On her way, she passes the high school. On the outdoor court, an older girl is practising shooting baskets. Hannah looks away from the basketball court and focuses on the road ahead of her.

On the next corner, Hannah sees two large boys standing in front of a small boy with a violin case on the ground in front of him. One of the large boys has his arms crossed over his chest and his head tilted to the side. Hannah remembers that Miranda Richards used to stand with her arms crossed over her chest that way.

At the beginning of grade six, Miranda teased me about everything: my lunch, my clothes … my being black.

Hannah squints, but she's too far away to make out faces. She wipes the tears away from her eyes. She takes a few more steps toward the boys. The smaller boy's shoulders are hunched and he's looking at the ground. He looks like a scared animal.

I wonder if I looked like that when Miranda picked on me. Is that why June stood up for me?

One of the larger boys takes a step toward the smaller boy and grabs him by the collar. Before she has time to think about it, Hannah is striding toward them.

"Max?" she says, recognizing the larger boy from her math class.

"Hey, Hannah!" says Max. Right away he steps back from the smaller boy.

"What's going on?"

"Nothing," he replies with a shrug. He motions at the smaller boy. "Me and Eli were just talking." Eli's mouth is clamped shut and his cheeks are bright red. "What's up with you?" asks Max.

"Just walking home."

"Have you been crying? Your eyes are all puffy," says Max's friend Johnny.

Max immediately elbows Johnny. "Not cool, man."

"What?"

"You don't point out to a girl that she's been crying. They don't like that."

"I'm betting boys don't like it either," points out Hannah.

"Right," agrees Max. "People don't like it." He looks right at Johnny. "So don't do it." Johnny nods. "All right, man. We should go. See you tomorrow, Hannah."

Max and Johnny walk down the street. Hannah doesn't move until they're out of sight. Neither does Eli.

He looks at the ground and mumbles, "Thanks."

"I didn't do anything."

"You didn't walk away." Eli reaches down to pick up his violin case.

"Do you go to Central Vancouver Middle School?" Hannah asks.

Eli nods.

"What grade are you in?"

Eli looks at Hannah, then at the ground, then back at Hannah. "Yours."

"Really?"

"Yes," answers Eli. His voice is quiet but annoyed. "I'm thirteen. Just because I'm short —"

"I didn't mean —"

"My birthday was in December."

"I've got a fall birthday," says Hannah quickly. "September. I get it. I hate when people think I'm younger, too. I was only asking because I don't recognize you."

"Oh."

"Do we have any classes together?"

Eli shakes his head. "I'm in French immersion."

"So how do you know me?"

Eli shrugs. "You're friends with June Kan. Everyone knows June Kan."

The two stand in silence.

"I'm walking home," Hannah says. "Which way are you going?" When Eli points in the direction of Hannah's house, she nods. "Me too."

Hannah and Eli start walking in the same direction, not quite together. Hannah is too upset to try to make any more conversation, so they walk in silence. Eli clutches his violin case tightly to his chest the entire time.

Hannah turns the corner. "This is my street."

Eli blushes. "Mine too."

"Really?" Hannah is surprised when Eli nods. "Did you know that?"

Eli shakes his head. Seven houses before Hannah's house, Eli turns down a driveway.

"I guess I'll see you tomorrow?" says Hannah.

Eli nods again. He turns to walk toward his porch, but then stops and turns back. "I hope whatever you were crying about today is better tomorrow."

"Thanks," Hannah says, surprised.

Hannah looks down the street at the little house she and her mom live in. She's never been more relieved to see her front door.

3 WHAT NOW?

Hannah sits in the middle of the room in math class. She idly taps her pencil against her notebook. It's been a week since the basketball tryouts. As she stares at the numbers in the textbook, she wonders if the feeling she has is ever going to go away.

Will I just be a little bit sad for the rest of the year?

The bell rings to signal the end of the day. Hannah slowly piles her books into her bag. With no basketball practice after school, there's no rush.

"Hey, Hannah," says Max as he strides out of class.

"Hi, Max," replies Hannah.

"He's said hi to you every day this week," says June. "So?"

"It's weird." June's eyes light up. "Maybe he likes you!"

"What? No." Hannah has thought a lot about Max and Eli since last week. What were they talking about? What would've happened if Hannah hadn't shown up?

Hannah and June get up and walk out of class together.

"Do you wanna hang out tonight?" asks Hannah.

"Maybe!" replies June. "I might be tired after basketball."

"Right."

"Hey! Me and some of the girls from the team are going to watch the senior high school team play on Friday. You should come with us."

"No, thanks."

"It'll be fun."

"But everyone knows I got cut from the team. It'll be weird."

"No, it won't. You like watching basketball."

"I used to."

"You still do. I'm sure of it. Besides, I'm turning fourteen."

"So?"

"February is my birthday month," says June with a big grin. "You have to do what I want all month."

Hannah laughs. "Is that how it works?"

"It is," says June with a wink. "I gotta get to practice. I'll talk to you later. And you're totally coming on Friday."

Hannah watches June jog down the hallway toward the gym. Hannah turns and walks in the opposite direction. It's easier to not have anything to do with basketball.

As Hannah wanders down the hall, she hears the sound of music. Someone is playing classical music that's bright and fast. Definitely not the sound of a guitar or a piano. Hannah is drawn toward the sound. When she reaches the music room at the end of the hallway, she can't help but poke her head in the doorway. Sitting alone in the middle of the room, Eli plays the violin. He's staring so intensely at the sheet music that he doesn't notice Hannah. She stands in the doorway and watches. He rocks back and forth and taps his foot to keep rhythm. Hannah closes her eyes to listen more closely.

Suddenly, the music stops. Hannah opens her eyes. Eli stares at Hannah but doesn't say anything.

"You're really good," says Hannah finally.

Eli blushes. There's a long silence. "Thanks. I've set a goal to make the orchestra next year. It's the hardest musical group to get into. So I practise. A lot."

"How do you set a goal?"

"Oh," says Eli. "Um … the goal can be anything that you want. And then you figure out how you're going to make it happen."

Suddenly, Max pushes past Hannah and marches into the room. Eli looks down and starts to pack up his violin.

"Eli, I've been looking for you." Max looks back at the door and recognizes Hannah. "Oh, hey, Hannah."

"Hi, Max."

"What are you doing in here? Shouldn't you be at basketball practice?"

Hannah's whole body becomes tight. "I got cut from the team."

"Oh," says Max. "That sucks."

"It does."

"I'm sure you'll make next year's team."

"Thanks." Hannah looks at Eli frantically packing up his case. "What are you doing here?"

"I was just looking for Eli," says Max. There's a lilt in his voice that makes Hannah nervous. "But it's okay. We can talk later. See ya, Hannah."

"Bye, Max."

Eli lets out a long, deep breath once Max has left.

"Is everything okay?" Hannah asks.

Eli opens his mouth a couple of times like he's about to say something. But each time, he stops himself. Finally, he says, "Yeah … Max's just bugging me."

"Like, we should be telling a teacher bugging?" asks Hannah.

"No!" says Eli quickly. "It's stupid stuff."

"Like?"

"He wants me to do his homework for him."

"And if you don't?"

There's a long silence. "I don't know."

I bet he does know, Hannah thinks. She remembers when she first became friends with June. June had stood up to Miranda when she was teasing Hannah.

"I don't like it," says Hannah honestly. She looks around the empty music room. "Wanna walk home together?" Eli's cheeks turn bright red. "We don't have to," Hannah adds.

"No, no. We can do that."

Eli and Hannah don't talk much as they walk. But it's not awkward at all. As they pass the high school, Hannah notices the older girl shooting baskets on the outdoor hoop again. The girl's movements are fast and purposeful. She shot fakes—pretending to shoot by looking at the basket and making the motion of a shot with her arms but without releasing the ball. Then, she does a drive, taking a dribble and exploding toward the basket. Her steps are firm, but she loses her balance near the rim and misses the shot.

"Ugh!" yells the girl. She runs after the rebound and does the move again. This time, she scores.

★★★

On Friday night, Hannah sits in the back of June's mom's car, squished between Taylor and June.

"I'm so excited to watch the game," squeals June.

"Me too," agrees Taylor.

Hannah doesn't say anything. Instead, she burrows her hands inside the sleeves of her sweatshirt. When June's mom parks, the three girls hop out of the car.

"Come on!" says June.

Hannah sighs. "I should never have let you talk me into this."

"Of course you should've. It's gonna be fun."

"I can't believe we'll be going here next year," Taylor says, looking around.

"Less than a year," says June. "It's February, and we start high school in September."

The girls walk to the gym. There are twice as many seats as in the middle school gym. They find a seat in the front row.

"So cool," says Taylor, as she watches the players warm up.

"Right?" agrees June. "Look at the uniforms. Purple, just like I said." June looks over her shoulder. "Check out all the people watching." She elbows Taylor. "This is gonna be us next year."

Hannah clenches her fists into tight balls. It would be so much easier to be at home. To not have to think about basketball. She recognizes the older girl from the outdoor court on the high school team. As the tallest player on her team, she is the most likely to win the jump ball, where the referee begins the game by tossing the ball into the air and two players from opposing teams try to tap it to their teammates. The girl stands in the centre circle where the jump ball takes place. The referee blows the whistle and throws the ball into the air. The girl jumps and taps the ball to her teammate, who passes it up the court to another teammate. The Vancouver City High School team scores!

"Who's that?" asks Hannah.

"Caroline Abram," answers Taylor, with wide eyes. "She's one of the best high school players in the city."

The whole gym cheers. After playing defence, the Vancouver City High team gets the ball. Caroline catches the ball at the top of the key, the area closest to the basket. She shot fakes and drives at the basket. It's the exact same move Hannah has seen her practise on the outdoor court. Caroline beats her defender and scores.

Everyone claps.

"She's so good," says Taylor in an awestruck whisper.

"Yeah," agrees Hannah.

As Hannah watches the ball zip around the court, her clenched fists slowly release. The game is dynamic and fast. She's sitting close enough to the court to hear the players call out and play as a team. By midway through the first quarter, Hannah wants nothing more than to play in this gym. For this team. Wearing the purple uniform alongside June.

Maybe Max is right. Maybe I could make next year's team.

On the court, Caroline scores a three-point shot just as the quarter-time buzzer sounds. The crowd goes wild.

But how am I going to do that when all the other players are practising and playing and getting better?

Hannah doesn't have time to let the thought upset her. The horn for the second quarter sounds, and the players are back on the court, ready to play.

4 THE DEAL

At lunch, Hannah sits in the cafeteria beside June. She looks down at her turkey sandwich.

"Yesterday's practice was really hard," laments Chantelle. She's on the basketball team with June. "My legs are still sore from all the running."

"I know," whines June.

June and Chantelle look at Taylor expectantly. Taylor shrugs. "We were goofing off. We deserved to run."

"Seriously?" asks June.

"We can't get better if we don't work hard."

"Fine," says June relenting. "You win this one, Tay."

I wish they'd talk about something other than basketball, Hannah thinks.

She looks up from her sandwich and stares out at the cafeteria. It's mostly filled with grade eight kids. There are a few tables of popular grade sevens in the corner. Then Hannah notices Eli standing at the door. He is completely still. Suddenly, he takes a step forward. He pauses. He looks nervous, as though he's peering into a cave looking for a wild animal. When his gaze lands on Hannah, Eli freezes for a moment. Then he raises his hand and signals for Hannah come over.

An excuse to stop listening to them talk about basketball practice? Yes, please! Hannah hops up and grabs her backpack.

"Where are you going?" asks June.

"To talk to Eli."

"Who's Eli?"

Hannah points across the cafeteria. "I'll see you in Math."

Hannah walks over to Eli. "What's up?"

Eli stands completely still. When he finally speaks, his words are rushed and quiet. "I want to make a deal with you."

"What kind of deal?"

"When you're around, Max doesn't bug me."

"Does he usually bug you?"

"You could say that," says Eli carefully. Eli's shoulders are slumped, and he looks down at his shoes. "But he's different around you. Like the other day, when you corrected him about boys crying. You looked him right in the eye, and he just … agreed with you." Eli says it like it's the most amazing thing in the world. "So … I want to …" Eli's voice shakes as he tries to finish his sentence. "… walk home with you. If you do it, then I'll help you."

"With what?"

"With whatever you want."

"I don't think I need help with anything." Eli looks to the ground. "Sorry."

"It's okay," says Eli, still looking at the ground.

The lunch bell rings, and Eli and Hannah separate to go to class.

In Math, Hannah glances at Max out of the corner of her eye. *What a jerk! I should've said yes to Eli's deal. But there's nothing I need help with.*

Hannah looks over at June. June is doodling herself in a basketball uniform in the margin of her notebook. *Except basketball. I want to make next year's team.*

Hannah suddenly remembers Eli practising in the band room.

"The goal can be anything that you want. And then you figure out how you're going to make it happen."

My goal is … to make the grade nine basketball team! Could Eli help me figure out how to make that happen?

The final bell rings.

June turns to Hannah. "Wanna come watch practice? Then you can walk home with me later."

"Can't," replies Hannah. "I've got plans."

"Oh," says June. "Well, I'll call you later, then."

"Cool," says Hannah. She walks down the hall to the music room. She sees several students packing up their instruments. But Eli keeps playing.

When he's finished his piece, he looks up. "What are you doing here?"

"I want to take you up on your deal."

"You do?" he says brightly. Then he looks away. "But you don't need help with anything. It wouldn't be fair."

"I need help with basketball. I ..." Hannah hesitates. It's the first time she's said it out loud. "I want to make the grade nine basketball team. It's my ... goal. And you seem to know about goals."

"I do!"

"So, we can trade. I walk you home; you help me with my goal. That's the deal."

Eli's eyes go wide. "Okay!" There's a moment of silence. "Let me pack up my stuff."

Eli and Hannah walk out of the band room to the front of the school. On the way, they pass Max.

"Hey, Hannah," says Max. He looks at Eli but doesn't say anything.

"Hi, Max."

"Headed home?"

"Yup."

"Cool."

"I'll see ya later, Max."

Max gives Hannah a nervous wave as she leaves the school with Eli.

"That was weird," says Hannah to Eli as they walk through the parking lot.

Eli's jaw is clamped shut. He takes long steps with his short legs. He doesn't speak until they're a block away from the school. "Max *is* weird," says Eli finally. "Also, he blushed."

"What?"

"When he waved goodbye, he blushed."

"So?"

Eli shrugs. "I think he likes you."

"Gross."

"I didn't even know Max could have feelings," says Eli. His tone is both playful and bitter.

"You really don't like him."

"You wouldn't either if you were me."

"Do you want to talk about it? We could tell —"

"You're walking me home now. So it's fine," says Eli quickly. "Let's talk about your goal."

"There's not much to say," says Hannah shortly. "I got cut from the team this year. I want to make next year's team."

"Why?"

"Does it matter?"

Eli turns bright red. They walk in silence for half a block before he answers. "Well, you can have a lot of reasons for wanting to do things. When you're goal setting, why you're doing something matters."

For the first time since tryouts, Hannah lets images of basketball flood her mind. She sees herself standing on a court surrounded by teammates. She closes her eyes and imagines taking the perfect shot. She feels the ball leave her hand, touching her middle finger last.

She hears the sound of the ball swishing through the net. When she opens her eyes, her body is filled with warmth.

"I miss being on the court with my friends. I miss sprinting to get back on defence. I miss the sound of the ball when it clanks against the rim. I miss the feeling of shooting the perfect shot."

"Cool."

"How is any of that cool?"

"There are lots of reasons to do something. It sounds like you play basketball because you love it. That's a good start for goal setting."

"So, I pass step one?"

"Totally."

Just as Hannah and Eli arrive at Eli's house, a car pulls into the driveway. Hannah is surprised to see Caroline Abram get out of the driver's seat.

"Hey, Eli," says Caroline. Caroline looks even taller up close than she does on a basketball court. Caroline looks at Hannah suspiciously. "Who are you and what are you doing with my little brother?"

Hannah's heart begins to pound. "I, uh …"

"She's helping me," says Eli quickly.

Caroline puts her hand on her hip. "Actually helping, or helping by not bullying you when you don't do her homework for her?"

"Hey!" says Hannah before she has time to think.

"Actually helping. She looks people in the eye and

she says what she thinks. Even with Max."

"I do?"

Eli nods and Caroline softens. "Okay." She turns to Hannah. "Sorry, kiddo. Gotta look out for my little bro." Caroline walks down the driveway and into the house.

"Your sister is Caroline Abram?" ask Hannah. Eli nods. "She's the best player in the city."

"Everybody says that," says Eli with a smile. He turns to walk down his driveway.

"Eli?"

"Yeah?"

"How do you know so much about goal setting?"

"My parents make me do it for orchestra."

"That's cool. If my mom didn't work so much, she could help me like that." Hannah pauses. "Why do you want to make the high school orchestra?"

Eli lights up. "The conductor is the best. And they have more rehearsals per week than any other band in the school. So I'd get to play more." Hannah smiles at Eli's sudden energy. He gets to his door but turns back to Hannah before he opens it. "I'll see you tomorrow after school?"

"For sure."

5 PLAYING WITH THE BOYS

Hannah and Eli walk out the school doors, past Max and his friends, and away from the school. Once they're out of the middle school parking lot, Eli turns to Hannah.

"So, step two of goal setting —"

"We don't always have to talk about my goal."

"Sure we do. That's the deal. We know why you want your goal," he says seriously. "Now we need to figure out what might stop you from getting it. That's the next step. What's the biggest thing standing between you and your goal?"

"I'm not playing like everyone else. They're all getting better, and I'm not."

"You need to play more?"

"Yeah, but there's no one to play with."

"That's not entirely true."

"What do you mean?"

"Meet me in the gym tomorrow at lunch. Be dressed for basketball."

"Why?

"You'll see," says Eli, as he turns to walk up his driveway.

The next day at lunch, Hannah stands at the gym doors. She's wearing her basketball gear for the first time since tryouts. The fabric of her shorts feels perfect against her skin. Hannah reaches out and places her hand on the door. She pauses and closes her eyes. She remembers standing on the other side of the door in front of Mr. Suto.

"I'm sorry, Hannah. You didn't make the team this year."

A shiver runs through Hannah's body. She turns away from the door and slams into Eli.

"Ouch!" says Eli, stumbling back two steps.

"Sorry … I was just … leaving."

"Why?"

"I can't do this."

"You don't even know what you're doing yet."

"I hear basketballs bouncing. People are playing."

"Exactly! There's a group of guys that plays at lunch. You can play with them."

"I can't."

"But you said not practising was stopping you from making next year's team."

"That's next year. Maybe it'll be easier to play by then."

"Maybe," says Eli. "But you said it yourself. How are you going to make next year's team if you haven't played? Making the team is your goal, isn't it?"

"Yeah, but …"

"But what?"

"I can't play with the boys' team."

"None of the guys are on the boys' team. They just play for fun."

"What if I suck?"

"Well … is it worse to suck now or to not play basketball next year either?"

Hannah takes a deep breath. Through the door, she hears a basketball clank on the rim. She looks down at her hands. She misses the feel of a basketball spinning against her palm.

"It's worse not to play next year," she mumbles finally.

Eli walks past Hannah and grabs the gym door handle. He pushes the door open and holds it. "Coming?"

"I guess." Hannah walks through the door. On the court, a group of boys stands around a hoop, casually shooting basketballs. Eli waves at one of the boys, who jogs over.

"You must be Hannah," says the boy. "I'm Luke. Eli said you might come."

Hannah turns to Eli. "You play basketball?"

"A big, hard orange ball being thrown at my face?" asks Eli, shaking his head. "No."

"Hey, man," says Luke. "You got other skills." He turns to Hannah. "You ever heard him play violin? He's crazy good. Best in our community orchestra. So,

Hannah, you wanna play with us?"

Hannah looks around. She's the only girl in the gym. "I dunno …"

"You said you needed to play more," says Eli. "They play every day at lunch."

"Come on," says Luke. "You can be on my team."

Hannah nods. Luke gathers all the boys together, and they pick teams. As promised, Hannah is on Luke's team, alongside Adam, Graham, Dan, and Ryan.

Luke starts with the ball, and Hannah can feel a tingling in her fingers. *What if I'm not good enough to be playing with the boys?*

"Game on," says Luke. He immediately passes the ball to Ryan on the wing, which is outside the three-point line near the sideline. Ryan looks inside to Adam, who towers over his check, or defender. Even though the pass is firm and direct, Adam struggles to catch the ball. He finally gets control of it. But he moves his feet before dribbling.

"Travel!" yells Adam's defender.

The game stops. Adam looks to Luke with wide eyes. Hannah cringes and waits for Luke to yell at Adam. But Luke just laughs. "Remember, man, you've got to dribble the ball before you move, otherwise it's a travelling violation."

"Right," says Adam seriously.

Joseph is on the other team. He dribbles the ball up the court. On every dribble, he bounces the ball between his legs, passing it from one hand to the other.

I can't do that, Hannah thinks.

When Joseph crosses the half-court line, he looks in Hannah's direction. Joseph passes the ball to Hannah's check, Vij, who catches it. Hannah nervously gets into defensive stance. Vij takes two hard dribbles to the right, but Hannah slides with him. He's forced to pass the ball away. Hannah sighs with relief.

On the other side of the court, a player shoots and misses. Luke grabs the rebound. He begins to charge toward the basket. Hannah runs alongside him. Just when it looks like Luke is about to score, he passes Hannah the ball. Surprised, Hannah fumbles the pass. She's wide open but is afraid that she will miss.

Hannah passes the ball to Adam. He catches it and throws the ball at the hoop. It clanks off the backboard and out of bounds.

"You should have taken the shot, Hannah," encourages Luke.

The game continues. Hannah gets the ball several times when Vij isn't anywhere near her. But the nervous tingling in her fingers stops her from shooting.

The boys stop for a water break.

"How's the game going?" asks Eli. "It looks good from here!"

Hannah shrugs. "Okay, I guess."

"You guess?"

"It feels good to play, but —"

"She won't shoot," interrupts Luke.

"Why not?" asks Eli.

"I might miss," Hannah admits.

"So?" Eli frowns.

"I'm the only girl."

"So?"

"Well, I don't want to be the girl who's missing all her shots."

"Have you been playing with the rest of us?" asks Luke. "Dan hasn't even hit the rim yet."

"Hey, man!" says Dan.

"It's not an insult. It's the truth."

Dan considers this. "Fair."

"Most of us didn't even try out for the boys' basketball team. And the guys that did all got cut. Including me."

"I'm sorry," says Hannah.

"Oh, it's fine. I just meant none of us care about being 'the boy who misses all his shots.' So why should you care if you miss some of yours?" Luke turns to the rest of the boys. "Come on, boys and girl. Let's get one more game in before the end of lunch!"

The other team starts with the ball. Joseph crosses the ball between his legs several times before he crosses the half court line. Hannah notices his check isn't near him.

Why is he just doing it? Just to show off?

Joseph stares in Vij's direction. As the ball leaves

Joseph's hand, Hannah lunges forward, knocking the ball forward. She chases after the ball and gains control of it. She starts to run and dribble toward the basket. Hannah looks up. She's on the right side of the basket.

No! I can't do right-handed layups.

Hannah looks over her shoulder. She's far enough ahead of the boys that she can cross over to the left side of the basket. She easily shoots a left-handed layup and scores.

"Nice!" exclaims Luke.

"Good job, Hannah," adds Adam. Hannah can't help but smile as she runs back and gets ready to defend.

★★★

It takes most of the class after lunch for Hannah to stop sweating, but by the time she gets to Math, she's finally dry. She slips into her desk beside June.

"Where were you at lunch today?" asks June sharply.

"Oh," says Hannah. "I was playing basketball."

"With who?"

"Just some boys."

"From the boys' team?"

"No."

June tilts her head to the side and stares at Hannah. "I guess if I get to play after school, it's fair that you play at lunch. Weird … but fair."

"Why is it weird?"

"I like to eat at lunch," says June matter-of-factly. "And be in the cafeteria with everyone. Didn't you miss us?"

Not really. "Yeah … totally."

"So, you'll be back tomorrow?"

"I don't know," says Hannah honestly. Before she can say any more, the math teacher starts the lesson.

6 CHALLENGES

Hannah strides down the hallway toward the gym and pushes through the door. She's been playing basketball at lunch with Luke and the boys for three months.

"Hey, Hannah."

"Hannah!"

"Yo, girl."

"Hey, guys," says Hannah. She sits beside Eli in the bleachers.

"Ready, Hannah?" asks Luke.

Before Hannah can answer, the gym door swings open. Suddenly, June is bounding across the gym floor.

"Hannah!" she squeals, running over to give Hannah a hug.

"What are you doing here?"

"We've got a big playoff game coming up and we wanted to get some extra practice in," says Taylor, striding in behind June. "June says you play at lunch?"

Hannah's heart is thumping in her chest. "Yeah."

"Can we play with you?"

"I guess," says Hannah. "If the boys are okay with it."

Luke nods. "Yeah, that's cool."

June and Taylor wave to the rest of the team to join them in the gym. They huddle together to chat before playing. Hannah starts bouncing her leg up and down.

"You okay?" whispers Eli.

"It's weird to have them here."

"Come on, Hannah," says Luke. "We're gonna need you."

Hannah gets up off the bleachers and joins the boys on the court. "All right, Hannah. Give us the scoop," says Luke. "Who are their best players?"

"Taylor's really good. You should probably guard her."

"Okay. Who do you want to guard?"

"I don't know," says Hannah. She looks over at the girls. Elsa was the weakest player on the starting lineup when Hannah was on the team. "Elsa?"

"Sounds good."

Once they've sorted out who each player will guard, Hannah and the boys walk onto the court.

"This'll be so much fun!" says June giddily.

"Totally," says Hannah, but her fingers are still tingling with nerves.

I've got to show everyone how much better I've gotten since tryouts, Hannah thinks.

The girls' team starts with the ball. Joseph defends Laura, the point guard who dribbles the ball from the defensive end to the offensive end. He reaches for the ball, but Laura easily avoids his swatting hand. She charges past Joseph. Hannah steps in to help. The moment Hannah leaves Elsa, Laura passes Elsa the ball. Hannah can do nothing but watch Elsa shoot and score.

The girls' team cheers. Hannah can't remember Elsa ever scoring before.

Joseph begins to dribble the ball up the court. He crosses the ball between his legs twice. Laura reaches out and taps the ball. Joseph scrambles to grab it. Once he's got it, he quickly passes the ball to Hannah. Elsa's in a defensive position that is better than any Hannah's seen playing with the boys. Hannah shot fakes. Elsa doesn't move. Hannah shot fakes again. Nothing. Hannah is forced to pass the ball to Luke. He drives at the basket and scores.

Hannah sprints back on defence. The boys struggle to keep up with the girls' offence, and Taylor loses her defender. She ends up alone directly under the basket. She scores.

Joseph takes the ball out of bounds after the basket and then passes the ball in bounds to the ball to Ryan, who immediately shuffles his feet.

"Travel!" yells June, who is checking him.

Ryan looks to the ground.

The girls take the ball. Laura dribbles the ball up the court. She passes to Taylor, who charges toward the basket. Taylor shoots, but Luke blocks her shot. The ball is loose. Both Hannah and June lunge for the ball, but Hannah gets there first. Hannah pushes the ball out in front of her. June chases Hannah, forcing her to run toward the right side of the basket. As Hannah reaches the key, she starts to do a right-handed layup. But she gets the footwork wrong. Off balance, Hannah is forced to throw a shot at the rim and misses.

"Good defence, June," cheers Taylor.

As Hannah watches the ball bounce away from the rim, all the air leaves her body.

I'm still not good enough, she thinks.

The game continues. Every time Hannah touches the ball, Elsa is close enough to stop her from shooting. But she's far enough away to stop Hannah from driving to the basket. Hannah is forced to pass and defend.

When the lunch bell rings, the girls cheer to celebrate their ten-point victory.

"Good game," says Luke to Taylor.

"You too," says Taylor. She looks at Hannah. "This was fun. I see why you do it."

Hannah runs out of the gym to get changed. She slips into English just before the bell rings. The class is doing a lesson on commas, but Hannah can't focus.

They're still better than me. Even Elsa, Hannah thinks as her stomach clenches like a fist.

★★★

Challenges

When Hannah walks into math class, June greets her cheerily. "Hey!"

"Hey."

"I don't get a hug?" says June.

"I just saw you at lunch."

"So?"

Hannah leans over and gives June a short hug.

"Basketball was super fun today."

"Yup."

"You know what's going to be even more fun?"

"What?"

"The team's year-end party. I'm hosting, so you're invited!"

"Your season isn't even over yet."

"It's still going to be awesome," says June. "You have to come. I'm going to invite the boys' team too. We could invite Luke. He's cute."

"Is he?"

June rolls her eyes. "Seriously?"

"I don't know. He's just … Luke. I see him every day."

"Maybe his hotness wears off over time?" says June, like she's considering a deep question. "Or maybe …" June's eye glimmer mischievously, "you're in love with the little kid."

"Eli? What do you mean, 'little kid'? He's thirteen."

"He looks like he's ten."

"He does not."

"Maybe it's because I'm fourteen now. Everyone looks younger."

"I'm thirteen still. Do I look younger?"

"You're distracting me from my point."

"There's a point to this?"

"Yes! I think you love Eli. That's why you don't think Luke is hot!"

"Don't be weird."

"You've been spending a lot of time with Eli. I hardly see you anymore."

"Because you're at basketball," says Hannah, annoyed.

"All right, class," says Mrs. Singh. "Everyone, take out your homework."

After class, Hannah meets Eli in their usual spot by the band room and they leave the school. Hannah kicks a rock as they walk down the street. Each kick makes her feel a little better.

"What's wrong?" asks Eli.

"Were you watching at lunch today? I sucked."

"You looked fine to me."

"I couldn't do anything. And the one thing I did do, I did wrong."

Eli stares at Hannah blankly.

"I missed my layup," she explains. "I'm not improving. Not like they are."

"Hmm …" says Eli. "Are you getting worse?"

Hannah thinks about how playing against the girls

felt different from playing against the boys. The boys often lunge to try and steal the ball on defence. Or they jump when Hannah shot fakes. Elsa was different. She never jumped or lunged. She was patient and disciplined.

And … was she forcing me to go to the right all the time? Hannah imagines Elsa standing, guarding her.

She was! She was always guarding me so I'd have to use my right hand. The boys never do that.

"I'm not getting worse," answers Hannah finally. "But the other girls are getting better and … smarter." She turns to Eli. "You said goal setting would help me make the team."

"It will," says Eli quickly. There is a long silence. He looks away from Hannah. "Maybe."

"What do you mean, 'maybe'?"

"Well, it might help you improve. But goal setting can't control other players. It's not a superpower."

"I know," says Hannah, frustrated. She kicks another rock. "I wish it was."

"I don't," says Eli brightly. "If I had a superpower, I'd want it to be something cool. Like flying. Or being invisible." Eli turns into his driveway. He looks over his shoulder. "You don't need a superpower to make the team."

"Feels like I do."

"What you need," says Eli, "is a more detailed plan. That's the next step in goal setting."

"It is?"

"I'll think about what should come next. You should too."

"What am I supposed to think about?"

"What you can *do* to make the team." With that, Eli disappears into his house.

7 HARD CONVERSATIONS

After dinner, Hannah settles into her favourite spot on the couch. Her missed layup replays over and over in her head.

"You okay?" asks Hannah's mom. "You're staring into space."

"I'm fine, Mom."

"If you say so." Hannah's mom leans down and ruffles her hair.

Suddenly, Hannah's phone buzzes. It's a text from Eli:

Got a plan. Can you come to my house?

Hannah types a reply:

Now?

Eli responds:

Yeah. If you can.

Hannah rolls off her spot on the couch. She throws on her shoes and walks to Eli's house. He is sitting on the front steps. Hannah plops down beside him. They sit in silence.

"I used to find this really weird," says Hannah finally.

"What?"

"Sometimes we're just quiet."

"Oh."

"June's never quiet," explains Hannah. "This is kind of nice once you get used to it."

"Thanks?"

Hannah laughs.

There's another silence. Then Eli says, "I think you should talk to my sister."

"No way! She's the best player in the city, and I'm no one." Hannah pauses and remembers the last time she talked to Caroline. "She's also kind of scary."

Eli rolls his eyes. "She's not."

A car suddenly turns the corner and rolls into Eli's driveway. "Look, she's home from practice."

"That's why you invited me over! You tricked me."

"I did," says Eli. He looks pleased with himself. He waves at Caroline. "Hey!"

"Hey E-Money," says Caroline to Eli. She points at Hannah. "Hey you, the girl who walks my brother home."

"It's Hannah," says Eli. "She's got something to ask you."

"No, I don't," says Hannah quickly.

"Yes, she does."

Caroline raises an eyebrow at Eli. She sits down on the step in front of Hannah.

"Okay. What's up, Hannah?"

Hannah doesn't say anything.

"She didn't make the grade eight basketball team," says Eli gently. "But she'd like to make the grade nine team."

"Ah," says Caroline.

"I've been helping her goal set. But it's not going as well as we hoped."

"How's that?"

Eli looks at Hannah pointedly.

"I've been playing with some boys at lunch," explains Hannah. "I thought I was getting better, but the girls' team came in today. I missed my layup, and I couldn't beat my check. It's the same. I'm the same."

"Ah," says Caroline again. "It's great that you're playing. That's a really important part of improving."

"Thanks."

"But I'm guessing that none of the boys you play with made the boys' team?"

"No."

"That's cool. You don't have to be on a team to love and play basketball. But it means they won't be as focused on skill development. If you want to play organized team basketball, you need to develop your skills."

"So I should stop playing with them?"

"Of course not," says Caroline with a laugh. "But you also need to work on your weaker skills. That's why I shoot around every day after school."

"I've seen you! On the outdoor court."

"I'm not great at jump shots, so I'm trying to get better."

"I don't know what to work on. Probably everything."

"I'm sure you have strong parts of your game and weaker parts. Just like me. Why don't you ask the grade eight coach?"

"Mr. Suto? He cut me from the team."

"Exactly. He'll know where you need to improve."

"I don't think I can do that."

"You can. Do it tomorrow."

"What?"

"It's easy to say you want something. But to achieve a goal, you have to take action. How about this? If you talk to Mr. Suto and find out what you need to work on, I'll help you with a workout plan."

"Really?"

"Sure. But it has to be tomorrow."

The thought of talking to Mr. Suto makes Hannah's palms sweat and her heart thud. "I'll think about it."

★★★

At lunch the next day, Hannah stares into her locker like it's a deep cave.

"What are you doing?" asks June. "Your lunch is right there." June reaches over Hannah's shoulder and grabs her lunch from inside.

"Thanks. I was just daydreaming."

"About boys? That's what I'm usually daydreaming about. Today, in Science …" Behind June, Hannah notices Eli standing in the hallway. A crowd of people strides through the hallway in front of him. He looks right at Hannah but doesn't say anything. "… you know?"

Hannah looks at June. Her face is filled with glee and hope.

"Totally," says Hannah finally.

Eli takes a tentative step forward so that he's standing beside June.

"What do you want?" June asks him sharply.

Eli turns bright red and looks to the ground. He looks back up at Hannah. "Mr. Suto."

"I don't think I can," says Hannah.

"I don't understand," says June.

"I was going to talk to Mr. Suto about basketball. I want to ask him about what skills I could improve."

"But he cut you from the team."

"I know that," says Hannah. "But he knows what I need to work on."

"That's really hard."

"It is." Hannah shakes her head. "I shouldn't do it."

"Yeah. Totally. Don't do it if you don't want to."

"But you do want to," says Eli suddenly. He hasn't looked up yet. "Because of … your goal."

"Would you come with me?" Hannah asks June.

"Now?"

"I have to do it now or I won't be able to."

"But it's lunch. I talk to people at lunch, and you play basketball."

"So you don't want to come with me?"

"Do you *need* me there?"

"No ..." *But I want you there.*

"Cool! Let me know how it goes," says June. She swings her backpack over her shoulder and takes off down the hallway.

Hannah watches her skip away and lets out a deep breath. *Well, that sucks.* She turns to Eli. "Will you come with me?"

"Of course."

"Thanks."

Eli and Hannah arrive outside Mr. Suto's office. Hannah clears her throat. She knocks on the half-open door. Inside the office, Mr. Suto turns his chair toward them.

"Come in, Hannah," says Mr. Suto. "Is there something I can help you with?"

"I ..." Hannah's mouth is dry. She clears her throat. "I really want to make the grade nine basketball team next year. It's my goal. I know I need to get better, but ..."

Hannah looks at Mr. Suto's face. He has the same expression he had when he cut her from the team. Hannah's breaths get shorter.

"You got this," whispers Eli from behind Hannah's shoulder.

She turns to look at him. Eli nods in encouragement.

"Hannah?" asks Mr. Suto.

Hannah steadies herself with a deep breath. "I need to know what I need to work on."

"That's a great attitude, Hannah" says Mr. Suto, suddenly smiling. "I can certainly help with that. Here," he says, reaching into his desk. He takes out a pad and paper. "I can help make a list with you. What do you think you need to work on?"

Hannah remembers playing against the girls at lunch. "I need to suck less at right-handed layups."

"Whoa! Is there a way you could frame that, that isn't negative?"

"I need to work on my right-handed layups," mumbles Hannah.

"That's better! When you're goal setting, your wording is really important."

"It is?"

"Yes. You want to word your goals in terms of things *to do* rather than things *not to do*. So, you want to improve your right-handed layups." Mr. Suto scribbles notes on the paper. "You could also work on your offensive moves."

"I know," says Hannah with a sigh. "My drive moves aren't great."

"How could you word that differently?"

"I need to improve my drive moves?"

"Good! You would also benefit from working on your shooting."

Layups, offensive moves, shooting. "Aren't those all the skills?" asks Hannah.

"No," says Mr. Suto firmly. "You're a strong defender and rebounder. If you improve your offensive skills, you'll be a more complete player."

Hannah nods. "Thanks, Mr. Suto."

"You're welcome!" He hands Hannah the paper. "Feel free to come back any time with more questions."

"Okay."

As Hannah and Eli walk away from the office, Hannah whispers, "I did it."

"Yeah, you did," says Eli brightly.

"I did it," she says with more force. *And now I get to work out with Caroline!*

8 SMART GOALS

After school, Hannah meets Eli in the band room. He's playing her favourite piece of music. It's classical music, but it sounds like a dance. The notes get higher and faster.

SCREECH!

Eli sighs.

"You sounded really good," says Hannah.

"Right up until that moment where I didn't."

"Don't be so hard on yourself."

"Easy for you to say," mumbles Eli.

"Yeah, it is," says Hannah looking Eli right in the eye. "You work stupid hard and you sound awesome."

"Thanks," says Eli. He pauses. "It's cool that you can say what you think."

"What do you mean?"

"Like right now. You told me what you thought like it wasn't a big deal."

"It *isn't* a big deal."

"For you."

"For you either. No one who doesn't suck is going to be mad at you for having opinions."

"What about the people that do suck?"

Hannah shrugs. "Ignore them? Who cares about sucky people?"

Eli smiles. "Good point. You know who doesn't suck? My sister. Ready to go meet her?"

"Totally!"

Eli packs up his violin. They leave the middle school and walk to the high school's outdoor court.

"Hey!" says Caroline when she spots Caroline and Eli. She looks right at Hannah. "I heard you were awesome today."

"I don't know about that."

"You went to the coach who cut you from the team. You asked him what you could improve. That takes courage."

Hannah can't help but smile. "Thanks."

"So, what did he say?"

"I have to work on my right-handed layups. And my offensive moves are weak." Caroline puts her hand on her hip and raises an eyebrow at Hannah's negativity. "I mean … he said I need to improve my shot and my drive moves."

"Okay," says Caroline thoughtfully. She walks over to her backpack and takes out a piece of paper and a pen. She turns to Eli. "E, have you given her one of these?"

Eli shakes his head. Caroline hands Hannah the paper and the pen. The paper reads: "SMART Goals: Specific, Measurable, Attainable, Realistic, Timed."

"It's great to have a goal and to work toward it. But the next step is breaking your goal down into smaller parts. Like, what does it mean to work on your right-handed layups?"

"I don't know," says Hannah, worried.

"That's right!"

"It is?"

"Totally. Good goals are SMART goals. S is for specific. How could you make that goal more specific?"

The second Hannah thinks about doing right-handed layups, she thinks about her feet. It feels like they're never in the right place. "I could work on my footwork."

"Great!"

"Also, scoring the layup."

"Good."

"The M is for measurable." Caroline continues down the list. "So, how can you measure that?"

"I don't know."

"What about with a drill?" Caroline moves so she's standing a step away from the hoop. She holds the ball near her right hip and stands with her left foot behind her right foot. Suddenly, she takes a step forward with her left foot. She uses her momentum to jump into the air. She extends her right arm and raises her right leg and easily scores the layup.

"You try."

Hannah takes the ball. She stands the way Caroline was standing. It feels awkward to hold the ball with her right hand. She moves it to her left side.

"Nope! You've got to do it correctly in order to improve."

"Okay." Hannah moves the ball to her right side. She takes a step forward with her left foot and jumps into the air, but she loses control of the ball.

"Good!"

"How was that good?"

"You did it properly. When you can do ten of those in a row with the correct footwork, you can take it back another step." Caroline demonstrates as she talks. "Remember, the footwork for a right-handed layup is left foot, right foot, left foot."

"Left, right, left," repeats Hannah.

"Okay, next is *A* — achievable. Does this seem like an achievable goal?"

"I think so."

"Me too. The *R* is for relevant. This is clearly a super-relevant goal. The *T* is for timed. So, you need to put a time limit on when you want to achieve the goal."

"Next week?"

"Waaaay too soon. How often do you plan on working out?"

"Five times a week?"

"Goal setting isn't just saying you're going to do

something. It's actually doing it. Can you work out five times a week?"

"Probably not."

"How about three times a week?"

"Okay." Hannah writes "three times a week" on her sheet.

"Great." If you're working out three times a week, when does it seem realistic that you could do ten layups in a row?"

"In a month? So, by the end of the school year?"

"Good. Put it on the sheet." Caroline looks at Hannah. "Now, for your drive moves. I think you should work on your shot-fake series."

"What's that?" asks Eli from the sideline.

"It's a series of offensive moves." Caroline takes the ball and stands under the basket. "You toss the ball to yourself by throwing the ball in front of you and flicking your wrists back toward yourself." Caroline demonstrates. The ball hits the ground a few feet in front of her and bounces back in her direction. She catches it. "First, you catch the ball and shoot. Then you catch the ball, shot fake, and drive to a layup. Then, you catch the ball, shot fake, and drive to a dribble jump shot. Have you ever done a dribble jump shot before?"

"No."

"It's where you take one or two dribbles toward the basket, but instead of doing a layup you jump off of both feet. You shoot when you're in the air. You'll do the whole series from six spots. You need to keep trying until you score a basket with each move from each spot. We'll time you."

"Now?"

"In order to track your progress, we need to know where you're starting."

"It might take a while."

"It should. You're not practising to get better at skills you've already mastered."

Hannah takes the ball and tosses it outside the three-point line. Like Caroline, she grabs the ball, turns toward the basket, and shoots. She misses her first shot and chases after the rebound. Hannah goes through the motion again. This time, she scores.

"Good job." Eli claps from the sideline.

Hannah moves to the next spot and shoots. She makes one shot from each spot and one layup from each spot. Hannah returns to the first spot for the dribble jump shot. She tosses the ball out in front of her. The shot fake is easy, but when Hannah stops to jump, she loses control of the ball. She sighs. "Don't stop," instructs Caroline. "Do everything full speed to keep moving. If you make it, you're chasing the ball. If you miss, you're chasing the ball."

Hannah tosses the ball toward the wing and squares up to the basket. She drives toward the basket and finishes with a jump shot. Her balance is better, but the shot misses. Hannah chases after the rebound. Under her breath, she mutters, "This is going to take forever."

"It doesn't matter," says Caroline. "You're going to finish it."

Hannah continues the drill. Her breaths become short, and as she gets tired, each shot is harder.

As Hannah scores her fifth jump shot, Eli cheers. "Good job, Hannah!"

"I still have five more spots," says Hannah, breathing heavily.

"This is why it's called working out," says Caroline. "Keep pushing."

Hannah finally scores the last jump shot in the series. Caroline stops the timer. "That took you fifteen minutes and thirty-one seconds."

"That's really bad, isn't it?"

"It's not anything," says Caroline, "except your beginning. Do that every workout."

Hannah nods.

"I think that's enough for today." Caroline strides off the court.

Hannah looks at Caroline. "I don't know how to thank you."

"How about this? You keep looking after my brother, and we'll call it even."

Hannah looks at the sideline, where Eli is sitting. "Deal."

9 THE PARTY

On a warm day in early June, Hannah sits in the school theatre for an assembly. The principal from Vancouver City High School stands at the front.

"Our high school is the biggest in the district. Our students come from four middle schools in the area. This means that there are more students and bigger classes," he explains.

Suddenly, something occurs to Hannah. *I'm not just going to be trying out against the girls from our middle school team. I'm going to be trying out against players from all the other teams too!*

The principal goes on: "There's also going to be more homework. It's never too early to think about time management."

Hannah feels a nudge against her ribs. It's June, holding out a folded piece of paper. It reads: Invitation: Girls' Basketball Team End-of-Year Party, This Friday!

June is beaming with excitement. Hannah whispers, "I wasn't on the team."

June whispers back, "It doesn't matter. It's my party, and I want you there. Plus, all the girls like you."

Hannah sighs. "I don't know."

"You're totally coming," says June firmly.

After the assembly, Hannah and Eli walk to the outdoor basketball court.

Hannah begins her workout as usual on the right side of the basket. She leans her weight forward, bounces the ball, and steps forward. Her feet feel balanced beneath her. She does the layup footwork, and then jumps into the air, extending her arm toward the basket. She shoots the ball with her right hand. But it doesn't hit the right spot on the backboard. The ball clanks off the side of the rim and away from the basket. Hannah chases after it. As she grabs the ball, she notices that Eli is taking his violin out of his case.

"What are you doing?"

"I need all the practise I can get this week. I'm going to play while you work out." He pauses and looks away. "Doyouwannacometomyconcert on Friday?"

"What?"

"My concert. Friday. Do you want to come?" says Eli again. " I know it's not part of the deal —"

"I'd like to come," says Hannah quickly.

"Really?"

"Yeah."

"Cool," says Eli. "It's at 8 p.m. on Friday. I'll leave you a ticket at the door."

Friday at 8 p.m. … June's party! Hannah looks up at Eli. He's smiling, just like June was when she invited Hannah to her party. *I can do both. I'll just leave June's early.*

Eli begins playing his violin.

Hannah takes the ball and looks at the rim. *Left. Right. Left.*

Hannah leans forward and completes the steps. She jumps into the air. This time, she focuses on the rim as she shoots. The ball falls through the mesh of the hoop. For the next hour, Hannah plays basketball with the sound of the violin echoing around her.

On Friday night at 7 p.m., Hannah stands in the middle of June's living room. She empties a chip bag into a giant bowl. Some of the girls from the basketball team have arrived, but mostly the house is empty.

"I'm so glad you're here," says June. "I'm going to hang out with you all night long."

"I have to leave soon," says Hannah.

"Why?"

"I'm going to Eli's concert. I'll come back after."

"Eli?" says June teasingly. "Is he your boyfriend now?"

"Don't do that," says Hannah seriously. *When did June start teasing me? When did she start caring so much about parties and boys?*

"Whatever," says June. "You'll want to stay once the party gets going. I know it."

Why did I wait until now to tell her? thinks Hannah. *I should've let her know earlier.*

"It's one of our last middle school parties," adds June.

"Yeah," begins Hannah thoughtfully. "It's weird that we're going to be in high school next year."

"It's awesome," corrects June. "Do you —"

The doorbell rings. June jumps up to answer it. Jeremy and some players from the boys' basketball team stand on the other side.

"You're here!" squeals June. She throws herself into Jeremy's arms for a hug.

The boys gather on the couch. More people ring the doorbell and pile into the house. June skips around, welcoming people. Hannah eats Cheetos alone.

Hannah looks at her phone. It's 7:35. *If the concert is at eight, then I should probably leave by …*

"Hey," says Max, sitting down beside her.

"Hey."

"Cool party."

"Yeah, it's —"

"Can I ask you something?"

"You just did."

June plops down in a chair beside Max. "Hey, guys!"

"Hey, June," says Max. "I was just about to ask Hannah something."

"Ooooh," says June, winking at Hannah.

"About the Loser," says Max, as though "Loser" is

someone's name. Hannah stares at him blankly. "The chump you walk home with."

"Eli!" says June. She bounces, like she should get a prize for remembering his name.

"What about him?"

"Why do you even talk to him?" Max pauses for half a second. It isn't nearly long enough for Hannah to answer. "Because he's a total loser."

Hannah clenches her fist. She checks the time. It's 7:40. *I have to go.*

She looks up at Max. He's still rambling about how uncool Eli is. June is giving Max her full attention.

Hannah moves to get up, but neither June nor Max budges.

"He is super weird," agrees June. "Why do you hang out with him, Hannah?"

Hannah is glad Max has finally stopped talking. "I have to go."

"What?" ask June and Max in unison.

"I told you that I was leaving."

"You can't go," says June.

"I'll come back."

"But I want you to stay," whines June.

"But I want to go," counters Hannah.

"Come on," says June, batting her eyelashes.

"Yeah, come on, Hannah," says Max.

Hannah looks down at her phone. It's 7:45. "I have to go!"

She gets up. Max and June don't move to let her out. Hannah squeezes in between them.

"You're coming back, right?" asks June.

"Maybe."

Hannah closes the door behind her. She starts to sprint. She looks at her phone: it's 7:48.

Come on, Hannah. Run!

10 CONSEQUENCES

As Hannah runs down the street her mind reels.

Why didn't I leave earlier? Since when does June agree with Max?

Hannah thinks about the way June has been acting. *She is only interested in boys.*

Hannah tries to remember when June started to change. *Was it on her birthday? Did she turn fourteen and become different?*

Hannah bursts through the lobby doors at 8:03 pm. There's a man standing at the doors into the theatre.

"Excuse me, my friend left me a ticket for the show."

"No latecomers," says the man. "It disturbs the performance."

Hannah looks down at her phone. "But it's only 8:03."

"As you can hear, the music has already started. I can't let you in."

Hannah slinks away from the doors and toward a corner of the lobby. She listens to the music through the doors. When the first piece of music finishes, the audience applauds loudly.

"In our next selection, there will be a solo by first violin, Eli Abram," announces a voice from the other side of the doors.

Midway through the piece, the orchestra quiets down and there is the sound of a single violin.

That must be Eli!

The music sounds perfect, just the way it does when he practises. Hannah hums along to the tune. As the notes get faster and higher, Hannah can't keep up.

SCREECH!

The whole theatre goes silent.

"Oh no," Hannah mutters under her breath.

The silence continues. Hannah wants nothing more than to be on the other side of the door. Slowly, the violin starts to play again. The sound is quiet and tentative. Eventually, the full orchestra starts playing again.

Tears well in Hannah's eyes.

I should be inside the concert hall. Why didn't I leave the party earlier? It wasn't like June cared if I was there. Once the boys arrived, she hardly talked to me. Why did I care so much about what June wanted?

When the concert ends, people stream through the doors. Hannah stands in a corner, waiting. She sees Caroline.

"Hey, Hannah," says Caroline. "Eli said you might come, but I didn't see you in there."

"I wanted to be there, but June wanted me at her party, and then Max started talking to me and …"

Hannah looks up at Caroline, who has her hand on her hip. Hannah remembers Caroline's words: "It's not just saying you're going to do something. It's actually doing it."

"I didn't plan ahead. I was late, so they wouldn't let me inside. It was my fault," sighs Hannah. As she says the words, something inside her shifts. There are a dozen ways she could've planned better. "I should've been here."

"Well, make sure you're there next time," says Caroline seriously. "That's all you can do now." Hannah exhales loudly. "You can go if you want," offers Caroline. "He's probably going to be a while."

Hannah considers this for a moment. "I'll wait."

Caroline nods approvingly. There's a moment of silence. "How's basketball going?"

"Good!" says Hannah. "I hit ten layups in a row the other day."

"Just like you planned." Caroline nods approvingly. "The next step is to change your routine to reflect your improvement."

"How do I do that?"

"Well, you could try and make more layups in a row, or you could time the drill to put more pressure on yourself. See how quickly you can make ten layups in a row."

"I like that." Hannah looks at the open doors. Members of the orchestra walk out to greet their families, but not Eli. "How's basketball with you?"

Caroline's face lights up. Hannah sees it's the same expression Eli gets when he talks about orchestra. "Good! I just made the B.C. provincial team."

"Congrats!"

"We practise during the summer. Which will be awesome. And I'm also coaching at some youth camps. So, all the basketball."

"You coach, too?"

"I like teaching basketball and helping people learn. I think one day, when I can't play anymore, I'd like to coach."

"Is that your … goal?"

"Long-term, but for now, my goal is to rock it on the provincial team."

Hannah looks at the doors again. Eli is the last person to walk out with his parents. His shoulders are slumped and he's looking at the ground.

Eli's parents walk up to Caroline, but Eli lags behind. "How's he doing?" Caroline asks.

"Not great," says Eli's dad. "He says he wants to walk home."

"Absolutely not," says Eli's mom. "He shouldn't be alone right now."

"I'll walk with him," says Hannah suddenly.

Eli's parents furrow their brows at Hannah.

"This is Hannah," says Caroline quickly. "She walks home with Eli from school."

"Right. We've heard about you," says Eli's dad. "That's very nice of you to offer, Hannah. But Eli can be a bit of a stick-in-the-mud when he's upset."

I said I was going to do it, so I'm going to at least try. "I'll ask anyway, if you don't mind?"

"Go for it."

Hannah walks over to Eli. Even when she's standing right in front of him, he doesn't look up.

"I heard the concert," says Hannah gently.

"You weren't there," replies Eli, his voice shaking with emotion.

"I was late, but I sat in the lobby and listened. I heard —"

"Me screw up."

There's a long silence. "I'm sorry."

Eli shrugs. "I want to walk home," says Eli quietly. "Alone."

"No."

"Please, Hannah … just … just leave me alone."

If I was upset, I wouldn't want to be alone. Not really. "It's … it's … it's part of the deal," says Hannah. "I walk you home. That's how it works."

"Right … the deal. Fine. I guess you can walk me home."

Eli waves to his family. Hannah and Eli walk out together. They don't talk the whole way home.

When they get to Eli's house, Hannah looks at Eli. There are tears in his eyes, and they make Hannah want to cry too. She knows she should have been there to support him.

"It sucks," says Eli through a loud sniffle. "I worked so hard, and I still screwed up."

"It was one mistake."

"And now, everyone's disappointed."

"No, they're not."

"Why do you care? You're only here because of the deal," sniffles Eli.

Hannah feels hear heart crack in her chest. *What would Eli tell me if I was the one who had made a mistake?* "It sucks that today didn't go as you planned. But this concert wasn't your goal. Your goal is to make the orchestra."

"Yeah, but —"

"No but," says Hannah firmly. "That's your goal. You'll just keep practising over the summer. You'll keep working. You'll improve. That's what you'd tell me to do."

"I guess."

"It's true, and no one is disappointed in you. Not your parents or Caroline. Not me."

"Okay," he says quietly.

"Okay," says Hannah firmly. "I'll see you on Monday for our last week of middle school."

Eli finally looks up. He's no longer crying. "Okay."

11 FORM DRIVE

Hannah sits on the couch. Her house doesn't have air conditioning. With Hannah's mom at work, the only sound in the house is a fan whirring in another room.

Hannah wonders if June is having fun on her holiday. She sighs as she gets up off the couch. She grabs her basketball and spins it in her hand. She worked out the day before. *But it'd probably be good to get extra workouts in.*

Hannah heads for the outdoor court. As she walks down the street, she spots Eli holding a garbage bag in his hands.

"Hey!" says Hannah from the road.

"Hi," says Eli brightly as he puts the bag in the garbage can. "Just doing my chores," he explains.

"Cool," says Hannah. There's a moment of silence. "How are you? I haven't seen you since the last day of school."

"I'm good. I was at band camp last week. What about you?"

"We've only been on summer vacation for two weeks and I'm already bored. June's away with her family at their cottage and Mom's at work all the time."

"But you're still working out?" says Eli, pointing at Hannah's basketball.

"Yeah. I'm actually working out more now that there's no school."

"That's awesome," says Eli.

He's so supportive. I miss that. "Thanks." There's a long silence. "I should get going."

"Yeah, for sure."

Hannah moves to walk down the street. But she turns and says, "You could come with me?"

"Oh … I don't know," sputters Eli. "I can't play basketball."

"Okay. I guess I'll see ya later then." Hannah takes another step.

"Wait!"

Hannah stops at Eli's voice.

"We're out of school," he says. "So you don't have to walk me home anymore. But I said I'd help you make the grade nine basketball team. My part of the deal isn't over yet."

"I guess not."

"I don't have to play, right? I could just come and cheer."

Hannah smiles. "Totally."

When Hannah and Eli get to the court, they find

Caroline standing under one of the baskets, sweat dripping down her forehead.

Eli leans to Hannah and whispers, "She's been working out every day that she doesn't have provincial team practices. They go to nationals in a few weeks."

"Cool."

Caroline sees Hannah and Eli. "Hey E-Money and H-Dawg!"

"H-Dawg?" asks Eli, raising his eyebrow.

"I'm testing it out," says Caroline, winking at Hannah. "What are you doing here?"

"My workout," says Hannah proudly.

"How's that been going?"

"Good. I'm getting faster with the timed part."

"Let me see your layups."

Hannah's heart pounds. "Okay." Hannah goes to stand at the top corner of the key. She holds the ball on her right hip and leans her weight forward.

Left. Right. Left.

Hannah charges at the basket. When she gets close to the basket, she takes off, looks at the backboard, and shoots. The ball hits the backboard and bounces through the rim. Instinctively, she grabs the ball before it hits the ground.

"So …" says Caroline seriously. "You *have* been working out. That looked great!"

Heat fills Hannah's cheeks. "Thanks."

"Do you mind if I watch you do your workout?"

"Are you kidding?!"

Caroline shrugs. "I like helping people with basketball. Especially people who work hard."

"I bet you're a good coach."

"Not as good as I want to be, but I'm working on it," says Caroline. "Now, let's see what you got."

Hannah starts her workout. She begins with her layups. Eli cheers while Caroline watches silently. When Hannah starts doing the shot-fake series, she notices Caroline furrow her brow in the corner. Hannah finishes her workout and stops the timer: eleven minutes and thirty-three seconds.

"Good job!" says Eli.

"Thanks," says Hannah, breathing heavily.

Caroline takes a step forward. "Have you ever form shot before?" Hannah shakes her head. "I noticed that your elbow points to the side on your shot. Form shooting is slow shooting that focuses on the mechanics of your shot. I think it would help."

"Okay."

"After you do your shot-fake series, take fifty form shots." Caroline steps to the basket and goes through the motions as she speaks. "To form shoot, you begin with your feet shoulder-width apart. Then you put your elbow in a C position so that your wrist is parallel to your biceps. Bring your non-shooting hand to the side of the ball for support. Extend your legs and your arms, and finish with your palm facing the ground." Caroline completes the motion. The ball swishes through the net.

"Cool," says Hannah.

"You try."

Hannah looks down at her feet to make sure they're shoulder-width apart. She bends her legs.

Make a C with your forearm and biceps.

Hannah places the ball on top of her palm and then, in one motion, shoots the ball.

"Good," says Caroline. "I want you to think about your elbow. Make sure it isn't sticking out to the side."

Hannah goes through the motions again. When she bends her elbow, it points away from her body. Hannah moves it to the right position.

"Great correction," says Caroline. "How does it feel?"

"Weird," says Hannah honestly.

"If you keep practising, it'll improve your shot."

Mr. Suto said shooting is one of the skills I need to improve!

"Have you ever heard of a cue word?" asks Caroline. Hannah shakes her head. "It's a word you use to help remind yourself of something you're working on."

"Like a goal?"

"Like a goal," says Caroline. "But instead of saying the whole goal, you use one word. When you're form shooting, instead of saying 'I'm improving my shot by keeping my elbow in,' you use one word to remind yourself. I want you to think of the word 'elbow' when you shoot."

Hannah nods. She lines up her feet, places her arm in a C-form, and put the ball on her palm.

Elbow.

Hannah adjusts her elbow. She shoots the ball. It falls smoothly through the mesh of the hoop.

"Good! Now do that forty-nine more times," says Caroline brightly.

"I can count," says Eli.

Hannah takes the ball and starts to form shoot. Even though the summer air is hot and the sun pounds against her skin, Hannah couldn't be happier.

12 TWO-ON-TWO

Hannah is on her way to Eli's house. The sun pounds against the pavement, and even though she's only walking, Hannah has already started to sweat. When she arrives, Caroline is packing a big bag into the trunk of her parent's car.

"H-Dawg!" says Caroline warmly. She shouts into the house. "Eli! Hannah's here!"

"Good luck at nationals this weekend, Caroline," says Hannah.

"Thanks. I'm excited about it."

"It's super cool. I wish I could do that one day."

"You could."

"No," says Hannah. "I'll be lucky to make the grade nine team."

Caroline stops packing. "Why so down on yourself?"

"June's at basketball camp this week. She says all the good players are there."

"And you're not?"

"Mom can't afford it," says Hannah quietly. "Which

sucks, but whatever. It's just … it's like last year. Everyone else is playing and getting better."

"Just because you're not at basketball camp doesn't mean you're not getting better."

Hannah shrugs.

Caroline takes a step forward and looks Hannah directly in the eye. "Basketball camp doesn't make a player better. Hard work does. You can't control what other people do. You can only control what you do. And so far, you should be really proud of what you've done."

Warmth fills Hannah's body. "Thank you."

"Any time," says Caroline seriously.

Eli bounces out of the house. After wishing Caroline good luck at nationals one more time, Hannah and Eli walk to the outdoor court together.

Once Hannah ties up her shoes, she turns to Eli. "Wanna rebound for me again today?"

"Okay," says Eli. "Because I was okay last time, right?"

"You were great."

"Except for those times I dropped the ball."

"It doesn't matter. It's nice to have a rebounder."

"Right. Okay."

Hannah starts her layups on the right side of the court. She scores ten layups in under two minutes. She continues with her shot-fake series and then moves to stand under the basket. She places the ball on her palm and bends her arm.

"Elbow," she mutters under her breath. She shoots. The ball clanks off the side of the rim. Eli extends his arms to grab the ball. He bobbles it as it hits his hands, drops it, picks it up again, and passes it to Hannah. "I can't believe we start school in two weeks."

"Scariest thing ever."

"Actually?" asks Hannah as she moves her elbow into a *C* shape.

There's a moment of silence. "Yeah." Hannah shoots and Eli focuses on catching the ball as it falls through the hoop. "Middle school wasn't the best," he says quietly.

"Because of Max?"

Eli nods. "But Max wasn't the only reason. I spent a lot of time playing violin. I didn't spend that much time with people."

"You want that to be different?"

"I dunno … I think so. Maybe."

"Hey!" says a voice from the street. Hannah turns. It's June and two girls Hannah doesn't recognize. One is much taller than the other. Right away, Eli passes the ball to Hannah and retreats to the corner of the court. June and the girls walk up to Hannah.

June gives Hannah a hug. "Missed you today."

"Thanks."

"This is Manjeet."

"Hey," says Manjeet, the taller of the two girls.

"I'm Joelle," says the shorter girl.

"They're from basketball camp. What are you

doing?" asks June.

"Working out."

"We should all play!" says June suddenly. "Half court two-on-two." She turns to the girls. "Just like in camp today."

"Okay," agrees Hannah, nervously. *They've been playing all day. What if I can't keep up?*

She remembers Caroline's advice: *"Basketball camp doesn't make a player better. Hard work does."*

"What are the teams?" asks Joelle.

"Me and June —" begins Hannah.

"Should be on different teams," interrupts June.

Hannah snaps her head to look at June. June shrugs. "We play the same position. It makes sense that we check each other. Plus, Manjeet won the shooting competition in camp today. She's on my team!"

Hannah tries to ignore her hurt feelings. She turns to give Joelle a high-five.

"Game to three baskets?" asks June.

Everyone nods. Hannah's team starts with the ball. Hannah's fingers tingle with nerves.

I can do this.

Joelle holds the ball at the top of the key. Hannah moves to get open. Joelle passes her the ball. Just like she does in her shot-fake series, Hannah looks at the rim and fakes a shot. June jumps into the air. Hannah drives past her and scores an easy layup.

"Nice!" says Joelle, giving Hannah a high-five.

"That was a right-handed layup," says June.

"So?"

"You can do those now?"

"I've been practising."

Joelle takes the ball at the top of the three-point line again. Hannah works to get open. This time, June is several steps back. Hannah looks at the basket.

Elbow.

She shoots and scores. A surge of pride blasts through Hannah's body.

June stares at Hannah.

Joelle starts with the ball again. When Hannah moves toward the ball, June is right on her hip. Joelle can't pass Hannah the ball, so she takes a dribble. Manjeet reaches out and swats the ball away from Joelle. Manjeet takes the ball outside the three-point line and passes to June. Hannah keeps her hands up, but June is fast. June charges toward the basket. Just when she's about to do normal layup steps, she jumps off two feet instead.

"Yes!" says June with a fist pump.

"Nice power layup!" says Manjeet, encouragingly.

"What's a power layup?" asks Hannah.

"We learned it in camp today," says June proudly. "And I just did one."

June takes the ball.

She's faster and more skilled than the boys. I need to give her more space, Hannah reminds herself.

Hannah takes a step backwards. June looks at the

basket but passes the ball to Manjeet. Manjeet makes a strong move to the basket. She scores a layup.

"Two to two," says June proudly.

June holds the ball again. Hannah stays back. June shoots. Instinctively, Hannah chases after the shot. It misses, and Hannah grabs the rebound. She takes the ball to the top of the key. June is forcing Hannah to the right. Hannah looks at the basket and takes two hard dribbles. Just as she's about to shoot, June reaches out and grabs her arm.

"Foul!" says Joelle.

"No way," says June.

"Way," says Joelle. "You held her."

June rolls her eyes. She looks to the corner, where Eli sits silently. "What do you think? Was it a foul?"

Eli looks around nervously. "I'm not a basketball expert, but I think you're not allowed to grab her. Is that right?"

"So, it was a foul," says Joelle matter-of-factly. "Our ball."

June huffs. Joelle takes the ball.

June is right on Hannah's hip again. In fact, she's so close that she's holding onto Hannah's shirt.

Hannah looks down at June's hand. "You can't do that."

"There's no ref," says June with a shrug. "And I'm playing to win."

"It's still against the rules."

June takes her hand off Hannah's shirt. "Happy?"

Hannah grits her teeth and nods. Joelle attempts to drive to the hoop, but she's off balance. Her shot clanks against the rim and bounces into Manjeet's hands. Manjeet grabs the ball and dribbles it outside the three-point line. She shoots. June and Hannah both chase after the ball. June gets the ball and makes a move to drive to the rim.

Hannah reaches her arm out to block the shot. *She's too fast. I'm going to foul her.* Hannah pulls her hand back.

June scores. She turns to Hannah, Joelle, and Manjeet. "We win!"

Hannah exhales loudly.

June holds up her hand for high-fives. "Good game! That was totally fun." Hannah glances down at her hand and realizes her fist is clenched. She opens her hand and gives June a high-five. "Yeah ... good game."

13 HIGH SCHOOL

Hannah stands in the hallway of Vancouver City High School. Students pound through the hall like it's a busy city street. Everyone has somewhere to go, and they seem to know exactly how to get there. Except Hannah. Hannah has no idea how to get to math class.

"Hey," says a quiet voice.

Hannah turns to see Eli. "Hey!"

"How's it going?"

"Okay. You?"

"Okay." Like Hannah, Eli stares at the crowd of people. "Is it just me or does everyone seem really … big? Not tall. Like … older."

"It's not you," confirms Hannah. "And there are a lot more people."

"Yeah."

An older boy bumps Eli's shoulder as he rushes past. "Don't stand still in the hall," shouts the boy over his shoulder.

"Sorry," whispers Eli immediately. "Sorry."

Hannah and Eli start walking down the hall together. Hannah recognizes Manjeet, from summer basketball camp. *Manjeet goes here too?* she thinks. *How many basketball players are there in this school?*

Hannah takes a deep breath and a tentative step forward.

"Where are you going?" asks Eli quietly.

"I've got Math. It's in room 217."

"Me too!"

"Cool. Do you know how to get there?"

"Not even a little." Silence. "But we're on the second floor, right?"

"I think so."

"It makes me feel better that we both think so." Eli stares at a door number. "This is 215. So, if the next classroom is 216, we're headed in the right direction." Hannah and Eli take a few steps forward. "Two-sixteen. This is good."

They arrive at room 217 and sit down in two empty desks in the middle of the classroom. Hannah looks around. She doesn't know anyone except for Eli.

"So, I was thinking ..." begins Eli, as they wait for the teacher to arrive. "Do you want to start up the deal again?" He turns bright red and starts talking quickly. "I don't need to be walked home. Caroline can give me a ride. But I was thinking, for the few first weeks, it would be good if I didn't eat alone at lunch. Being alone at lunch is like standing in the spotlight. So, maybe I could eat with you? And I'll help you with basketball."

I'm going to need all the help I can get, Hannah thinks. "Sure. Where's your locker? I can meet you there at lunch."

"Near the science classrooms?" asks Eli tentatively.

"I don't know where the science classrooms are. Why don't we meet outside this classroom?"

The math teacher walks in. She tells them her name is Mrs. Himura and begins the class right away.

Mrs. Himura goes through the material so quickly, Hannah's hand cramps trying to take notes. The same thing happens in her next class and the class after. When the bell rings for lunch, Hannah's brain is ready for the break.

As she walks to meet Eli, Hannah's phone vibrates. It's a text from June:

Meet me in the cafeteria!

Hannah spots Eli. "Would you mind going down to the cafeteria? June wants me to meet up with her."

Eli bites his lip and looks to the ground. "I don't know … They probably won't even let me."

"What do you mean, 'let you'? You're eating."

"You wouldn't get it." Eli's shoulder are slumped and he's looking at the ground.

Hannah suddenly remembers eating lunch before she became friends with June. She would sit in front of her locker, eating a sandwich, alone. Hannah looks at

Eli. *If he won't go, I'll eat here with him.*

"We can just—" Hannah starts.

"No," says Eli suddenly. "I can do this."

"Are you sure?"

"No," says Eli. Hannah laughs. "But it's not fair to take you away from your friends. That's not part of the deal." Eli looks to the ground. "And I was thinking over the summer. High school has to be different. That's my new goal."

"Over making orchestra?"

"No! It's my … second goal. Make high school different. I can eat in the cafeteria," says Eli with more confidence. "Besides, you'll be there."

"So?"

"So I'll be okay."

When Hannah and Eli arrive in the cafeteria, they find June sitting at a table with a lot of others. Hannah recognizes Taylor and Max, but they're at the far end of the table. Everyone else is new. June waves excitedly.

"Hey!" says June. She leaps up from her seat to give Hannah a hug. "How was your first day? I've met so many people." She signals at the table. "High school is going to be so fun. Don't you think?" Hannah opens her mouth to respond, but June cuts her off. June turns to the table. "Everyone, this is Hannah."

"Hi, everyone," says Hannah. Hannah turns. Eli is standing three steps behind her. "This is Eli."

Eli manages to raise his hand in a wave. June tilts her

head and furrows her brow as she stares at Eli. "Come sit with me, Hannah!" she says finally.

Hannah sits down beside June, but there's no room for Eli. "Can you move over?"

"Why?"

"Eli's eating with us."

"He is?"

"I don't have to," mumbles Eli. He is staring down the table. Hannah follows his gaze. At the other end of the table, Max is eating his lunch.

"Don't be silly," says Hannah to Eli. She turns to June. "Move over." June scoots over. Eli hesitates.

"Remember your second goal," she whispers.

Eli slowly sits down.

At the table, June directs the conversation, and everyone is happy to follow. Midway through lunch, Luke walks up to the table. "Hannah! Eli!"

"Hey!" says Hannah. Luke's chest is wider than it was last year. There are dimples in his cheeks when he smiles. Hannah feels a zing run through her body. A blush fills her cheeks.

"Did you grow over the summer?" she asks finally.

"Four inches."

"Cool," says one of the other boys.

"I grew too," says Max suddenly.

"It's actually the worst," whispers Luke to Hannah, when everyone turns away from him. "It's like … I don't even know … My feet aren't attached to my body.

I tripped up the stairs earlier. Up. The. Stairs. I didn't even know that was a thing." Hannah and Eli laugh. "Anyway, some of us are going to play ball after school. Like last year at lunch. Only not at lunch. Wanna join us, Hannah?"

"Totally," says Hannah.

"Cool," says Luke. "How's the first day going?"

"Good, I guess? I don't know … I've got more homework today than we had in a week last year."

"Tell me about it. What about you, Eli?"

"Okay," says Eli quietly.

"You gonna join us after school? You can sit and watch like last year."

"I can't," says Eli. "I've got to practise if I'm going to make orchestra."

"When are your auditions?" asks Hannah.

"Not until November."

"Same as basketball tryouts."

"I'm already nervous."

Hannah glances down the table at Taylor. "Me too."

"Well, you're both welcome to join us any time," says Luke. He stands back up and walks away from the table.

"We're all going for ice cream after school!" announces June. Everyone nods in agreement. She turns to Hannah. "I don't want to hear it. You're coming."

"I haven't said anything yet."

"I know what you're thinking. You want to play

basketball with Luke. But it's the first day of school. We've got to celebrate and make friends. You can play tomorrow."

But I want to play today, thinks Hannah.

"Come on." June pouts. "For me?" She bats her eyelashes, like Hannah is some boy June is trying to flirt with.

I don't like that, decides Hannah. She looks around at the crowd of people. *But now isn't the time to talk about it.*

"Well?"

Maybe it'll be better to hang out with June. Then I can go home early and do my homework. Hannah sighs. "Okay. But just today."

14 OVERWHELMED

Hannah shivers as she chases the ball on the high school's outdoor court. The sun is already setting, and the orange ball stands out in the dimming light. Hannah grabs her rebound and tosses the ball out in front of her. She bounces the ball with her right hand and explodes forward. She scores the layup.

"Nice!"

Hannah looks up. Caroline stands on the edge of the court.

"Thanks!"

"It's getting dark. It's time for you to call it a day."

Hannah sighs. She jogs to her phone to check the time. "It's only seven o'clock."

"Come on, we can walk home together." Hannah joins Caroline. "So, how have the first six weeks of high school been?"

"Okay, I guess."

"You guess?"

"Well, my birthday was a couple weeks ago. That

was good …"

"But?"

"But other than my birthday, high school has been a lot of work."

"Ah," says Caroline.

"I've been doing my homework right after school …" Hannah stops. She doesn't want to tell Caroline it's taking hours to do her math homework every day. "My goal is to do three workouts a week."

"That's great."

"But now that it's getting darker earlier, it's hard to get my workouts in at night. I only got one day in last week."

"Goals aren't always easy. Sometimes, what was realistic when you set your goal isn't realistic anymore."

"What do you mean?"

"When you started goal setting you were in middle school. High school is harder. Maybe working out three times a week is too much."

"No," says Hannah firmly. "I can do it."

Caroline looks at Hannah seriously. "Part of goal setting is adjusting your planning for new circumstances. It's no different than adding to your workout when you improved."

"It feels different."

"Take a look at your schedule. Maybe there's another place you could find time for workouts. Get creative. Goal setting means adjusting all the time."

They arrive at Caroline and Eli's house. Caroline turns up the driveway. "And keep eating lunch with my little brother. You and I gotta keep that boy out of trouble," says Caroline with a wink.

Hannah walks to her house.

How can I get creative with my schedule? She wants to think about it more. But the moment Hannah walks in the door and sees the couch, she can't help but lie down on it.

"Long day?" asks Hannah's mom with a laugh.

"Every day is long," replies Hannah, snuggling into her favourite spot.

★★★

The next day at lunch, Hannah sits in the cafeteria, bouncing her knee up and down.

June puts her hand on Hannah's leg. "What's up with you?"

"Just thinking."

"About?"

"I'm not getting enough basketball in." The lunch table looks at Hannah. "I've been practising on my own, but not enough. I've got no time to play with the boys. It's hard with all the homework." Everyone nods in agreement. "Math is the worst."

"Math is totally brutal," says June.

"Don't do your homework," suggests Max from the

far end of the table.

"What?" says Hannah.

"Life is about priorities. Which is more important to you: math or basketball?"

"Basketball."

"So, there you go."

Hannah looks around at the table. Everyone is nodding in agreement with Max.

"But what if there's a pop quiz?"

Max shrugs. "You can cheat off the person next to you."

"I'm not a cheater."

"Whatever. It's just Math. I do it all the time."

Hannah rolls her eyes.

"One day won't matter," says June.

"Totally," agrees Dara, one of June's new friends.

"I guess. I mean, if I don't do my math homework, I could play with Luke and the boys after school. I can still get the rest of my homework done."

"For sure," agrees Max.

Hannah looks over at Eli. He is sitting straight up and shaking his head, but he doesn't say anything.

After school, Hannah pauses outside the gym doors. She can feel the weight of her math book in her backpack. *Maybe June and Max were right*, she thinks. *One day of missed homework won't matter.*

She walks through the doors.

"Hey, Hannah!" says Luke as soon as he sees her.

Hannah notices that heat fills her cheeks when Luke smiles at her. *That's new*, she thinks.

Hannah tears her eyes away from Luke. Several of the boys from lunch are there, but there are some boys she doesn't know. "Come on," says Luke, seeming to read her mind. "I'll introduce you to everyone."

After Hannah meets the new boys, they step onto the court. Hannah is on Luke's team. He wins the jump ball and tips it to Hannah. One of the boys swats at it, but Hannah holds the ball tightly to her hip. It feels so good to be playing alongside other people instead of standing on a court alone.

Hannah looks up the court to a boy name Bryce. But just as she's about to pass the ball, Bryce's defender reaches out his hand. Hannah is forced to stop and wait for Luke. She passes Luke the ball. Hannah jogs up the court. But by the time she's made it to the three-point line, her team has already shot. Hannah's lungs aren't used to running like this. By the first water break, she's breathing heavily.

After the water break, the teams go back on the court. The first time down the court, Hannah gets the ball on the wing. She shot fakes. Her check, Damian, lunges, and Hannah drives past him. Another player steps in to help Damian and stop Hannah. Spooked, Hannah picks up the ball and takes another step.

"Travel," yells one of the boys.

Hannah puts the ball down and runs back on

defence. *That was stupid!* she tells herself. *It's not like working out alone. There are other players on the court!*

When the game ends, Hannah takes off her shoes in the bleachers.

"Good game," says Luke. "It was nice to have you back."

"I've really missed playing with other people. Obviously."

"What do you mean, 'obviously'? You looked great out there."

"I've got to be better," says Hannah.

"If you say so," says Luke. Hannah gets up to leave. "See you tomorrow?"

"Absolutely." She leaves the gym and walks home.

When she passes Eli's house, Eli suddenly darts out of his door. "Hey!"

"Hey," says Hannah, as Eli runs toward her. "What's up? Is something wrong?"

"No," says Eli. "Well, kind of."

"Okay …"

"You were just playing basketball, weren't you?"

"Yeah … so?"

"So, you haven't done your math homework yet?"

"I don't think I'm doing it today."

"That's the worst idea … ever."

"It's only one day."

"You're only saying that because June said it," says Eli. Hannah is surprised. Eli is speaking with more force than she's ever heard from him before. "And you're already struggling to keep up."

"Hey!"

"You say it every day in class," points out Eli. "If you don't do your homework today, you'll fall behind, and you won't be able to catch up. You can't play basketball if you're failing a course."

"I won't fail," says Hannah. But now she feels unsure. "I don't think."

"It's a bad idea."

"But my math homework is taking me hours," stresses Hannah. "You should've seen me play today. I'm out of shape. And it's different to be on the court with other people. I've got to play more."

"Find another way."

"Like what?" says Hannah defiantly.

Eli scrunches his eyebrows together. He looks up at the sky and then back at Hannah. "I don't know."

"Well, that's not part of the deal."

Eli exhales loudly. He looks Hannah directly in the eye. "If you're going to cut corners so that you can achieve your goal, then our deal is off."

"What?"

"Why should I help you if you aren't really committed to your goal? Cutting corners isn't being committed."

"So you're not going to eat lunch with us tomorrow?"

"I don't know," says Eli. "Are you going to do your homework? Or are you going to let yourself fall behind because your friends gave you the worst advice ever?"

Since when does Eli stand up to people? wonders Hannah. *Am I … part of his goal? Is he right? Did June and Max give me bad advice?*

Eli turns and walks back his house. Hannah is left standing in the middle of the road, her heavy backpack tugging at her shoulders.

15 NO DEAL

As Hannah walks into math class, her eyelids droop. It feels like there are little weights attached to them. Hannah sits at her desk and slowly reaches into her backpack.

Eli slips into the desk beside her. Hannah doesn't look at him. *How dare he threaten to call off the deal! I should un-invite him from lunch. Where would he be with his second goal then?*

Eli stares at Hannah like she's a puzzle. Hannah can feel his eyes looking at the tired sag of her body. But before he can say anything, Mrs. Himura begins her lesson.

"Homework check!" she announces.

The class groans. As Mrs. Himura walks around the classroom, some students cower at their desks. The teacher shakes her head in disappointment. When she walks by Hannah's desk, she peers down at Hannah's open notebook.

Hannah's heart pounds in her chest.

"Good work, Hannah," says Mrs. Himura, scanning the page. "I can see you're struggling with some of the harder questions, But you did them all."

A smile creeps onto Eli's lips. When the teacher walks away, he turns to Hannah. "That's why you're so tired, isn't it? You stayed up to do your homework."

"It took me forever," sighs Hannah. "But I thought about it. I don't want to be someone who doesn't do her homework. And I really don't want to be someone who doesn't do her homework because her friend gave her stupid advice."

"I was thinking about your schedule," says Eli. Hannah feels a pang of guilt for being so mad at Eli earlier. "What if you asked Mrs. Himura for extra help so that your homework doesn't take so long?"

"She's kind of scary."

"No, she's not. It's the math that's scaring you. What do you have to lose?"

Hannah thinks about this for the rest of math class and part of English class. Eli's right. *If I want to play basketball, I have to figure out Math. Max's idea was stupid. Why did June listen to him? Why did I listen to June?*

Hannah replays the last day over and over in her head during her morning classes. *Lunch with June and Max. Playing basketball after school. Eli running out of his house.* Hannah's thoughts suddenly change direction. *He ran out of the house. He was waiting for me! Because … because he cares about my goal … About me.*

Hannah remembers the look on Eli's face when he threatened to call off the deal.

And he stood up to me, even though he knew I might get mad. He's meeting his second goal!

She looks at Eli. *Good for him … and lucky for me.*

Hannah starts replaying the day in her mind again.

By the time the lunch bell rings, Hannah's made two decisions. She walks to the cafeteria, where Eli is waiting outside the doors.

"I'm not eating in the cafeteria today." she says.

"Why not?" asks Eli tentatively.

"I'm going to ask Mrs. Himura for help with Math."

"That's great!"

"Also, I'm calling off the deal."

"What?" says Eli. The colour drains from his cheeks.

"I don't want to eat lunch with you because of some stupid deal. Or because of your goal to make high school better. I want to eat lunch with you because you're my friend."

"Really?" Eli blushes. "I mean … you're my friend too."

Hannah looks into the cafeteria. Max is telling a story and June is listening attentively. "You might actually be my best friend," she admits.

"What about June?"

"June's my best friend, but you're a better friend. At least, you've been a better friend lately. I haven't totally figured it out yet."

"That sounds like a big thing to figure out."

"Yeah," says Hannah. She sighs. *If Eli can have two goals, so can I. Goal number two: figure out my friendship with June.* "Wanna meet me after Mrs. Himura's class? We can eat lunch after."

"Sure."

★★★

Hannah packs up her books after a lunch session with Mrs. Himura.

"Thanks for your help," says Hannah to Mrs. Himura.

"You're welcome. It's been great to see you every day this week. You're working really hard, Hannah."

"I know I'm not getting all the questions right on the quizzes. But my homework is taking me half as long."

"That's great," says Mrs. Himura.

Eli is waiting for Hannah outside the classroom. They walk to the cafeteria together.

"Hey!" says June, hopping up to give Hannah a hug. "We missed you."

"You've missed me every day this week."

"Now that you've got a new schedule, I never see you."

"I thought it was too late to switch classes," says Dara.

"It's not that kind of schedule," explains Hannah.

"I'm getting help with Math at lunch so that I can play basketball after school."

"Cool."

"You could come and play after school," offers Hannah to June.

June shakes her head. "Some of us are hanging out after school. And I don't need to practise to make the team."

It's like June's words fly through the air and land in Hannah's stomach. She feels like she's been punched.

Beside Hannah, Eli coughs.

"Did you say something?" says June sharply, turning to Eli.

Eli looks down at this lunch. "That wasn't a very nice thing to say." His words are quiet but forceful.

June glares at Eli. Then she looks at Hannah. Hannah looks away.

"Sorry," says June. "I didn't mean —"

"It's okay," says Hannah quietly.

June takes a bite of her sandwich. Hannah looks down at her apple. Suddenly, she doesn't feel very hungry.

★★★

After school, Hannah walks to the gym. When she gets to the door, she pauses, remembering June's words.

"You planning on opening that door?" asks Luke.

"Sorry," says Hannah.

"All good." He opens the door for them both, and Hannah's heart melts a little. Then she looks at the basketball hoop. She sighs.

"You okay?" Luke asks.

"Just thinking."

"About?"

"Basketball."

"Well, this is a good place for that."

Hannah and Luke are the first people in the gym. After putting on her basketball shoes, Hannah grabs a ball and starts shooting on one of the empty nets.

June's right, Hannah thinks. *I got cut from last year's team. I do have to practise.*

Luke comes and rebounds for her. "What were you thinking about basketball?"

"I'm not as good as the other girls."

"You're plenty good."

"Thanks. I've been working super hard. But I still might not make the team."

June hasn't worked at all and she probably will *make the team. That sucks*, Hannah thinks. *Elbow.*

She readjusts her elbow. She makes four shots in a row.

"I won't make the boys' basketball team," says Luke suddenly. "But I'm going to tryouts anyway because I love to play."

"I love to play too." Hannah takes a step back so

that she's just outside her shooting range. Her first shot clanks against the rim.

Elbow.

The shot hits the back side of the rim and goes through the basket.

"So, you have to work harder than everyone else," says Luke. "You're also doing the thing you love more than anyone else."

"Taylor practises on her own too."

"More than most people."

"True."

Hannah thinks about it. *It still sucks that June said that. But Luke's right. I love to play, and I've played more basketball than almost anyone this year.*

Hannah catches the basketball and takes another shot. It falls easily through the mesh of the hoop. More boys pile into the gym.

And I get to play again today.

16 NERVES

It's November, the week before basketball tryouts. Hannah bounces her pencil up and down against the desk in one of her afternoon classes.

What if I don't make the team? Left. Right. Left. Keep my elbow in when I shoot. What if I don't … keeps running through her mind.

"Does anyone have any questions about the homework?"

Hannah's head shoots up. *Homework?*

The bell rings. Hannah turns to William, the boy who sits behind her. "What was the homework?"

"Read pages fifteen to thirty-five of the textbook."

"Fifteen to thirty-five. Got it. Thanks."

"You nervous about something?"

"What? Why would you say that?"

"Your leg was bouncing up and down all class. It was shaking my desk."

"I'm sorry."

He shrugs. Hannah packs up her books and goes to

her locker. June is leaning against the locker beside hers.

"Big news!"

"What's that?"

"My parents are going away this weekend, so I'm having a party on Friday."

"Do they know?"

"Sort of," says June mischievously. "They know I'm having some people over."

"I think I have something Friday."

"Cancel it. This is going to be our first real grade-nine party."

"Hey, June," says Max. "Hey, Hannah. You hanging out with us after school?"

"No I gotta play —"

"Basketball," say June and Max in unison.

"We know," adds June. "Come on, Max. Let's go meet everyone."

Hannah looks in her backpack. She grabs an apple and takes a few bites, but the butterflies in her stomach are flapping too hard. She puts the apple away again. Hannah strides from her locker past the gym to the band room, where Eli is practising. Hannah pauses and listens to the notes drift through the air. Eli easily speeds through the sections that used to challenge him.

When he finishes the piece, Hannah interrupts. "You sound great, and I'm freaking out."

Eli stops playing. "About?"

"Basketball tryouts. I can't eat. I can't focus.

Apparently, I spent all of Social Studies bouncing my leg up and down. I'm freaking out."

"Honestly, I'm freaking out a little too. My auditions are this Friday."

Right, that's what I'm doing Friday, Hannah realizes. "Well, you sound really good," she says.

"I don't know."

"Last year, you couldn't play thirty seconds of that piece without making a mistake. Now you can play the whole thing."

"I guess …"

"I don't even know if I can catch a basketball right now I'm so nervous about tryouts."

Eli narrows his eyes. "You think I'm getting better because you can hear my progress …" He begins. "How can you track your progress?" There's a long silence. "Your workouts! They're timed, right?"

"Yeah."

"Go do your workout and time yourself. Then, go find your very first workout sheet."

"Okay."

"Go!" says Eli, shooing Hannah away with his hand.

Hannah stands on the outdoor court and reads her first goal-workout sheet aloud. "Layups. Do ten in a row from one step away and then step back."

Right. I used to not be able to do a full layup.

Hannah stands on the wing. She looks at the basket.

Left. Right. Left.

Hannah dribbles the ball and explodes forward. When she gets to the rim, she jumps into the air and easily places the ball against the backboard. She scores! Hannah grabs the ball and returns to the wing to shoot another layup. She scores again. It's not very long before she's scored ten in a row.

She starts her timer for the shot-fake series. Within minutes, she's completed the layups and shots. For the jump shots, Hannah tosses the ball out to the wing, squares up to the basket, drives, and then pulls up and jumps directly into the air. As she shoots, she pulls her elbow in and looks directly at the basket. The ball swishes through the hoop. When she completes the drill, she's breathing heavily. She jogs over to her phone to stop the timer: eight minutes and thirty seconds.

Hannah looks down at her first goal-setting sheet: fifteen minutes and thirty-one seconds.

Whoa! That's almost twice as long. I guess I really have improved!

She looks at the sheet again. At the top, it reads: "Goal: Make the grade nine girls' basketball team."

As Hannah thinks about tryouts, she feels the butterflies in her stomach. But they aren't flapping nearly as hard as they were before she did the workout.

★★★

On Friday afternoon, Hannah stands completely frozen. She stares at a large sign posted on the cafeteria door: Grade Nine Girls' Basketball Tryouts Next Week!

"I can't believe tryouts are here already," says Taylor.

"Me neither," says Hannah.

"I'm not gonna lie. I'm a little nervous."

"You don't have anything to be nervous about," says Hannah honestly. "You'll make the team for sure."

The girls continue to stare at the poster. "You going to June's party tonight?" asks Taylor.

"I don't know. You?"

"No," says Taylor firmly. She leans in to Hannah's ear. "I think some of the boys are going to bring alcohol."

"Does June know? Her parents would freak out."

"It's Max. She knows."

"Right," says Hannah. *Since when does June hold parties where there was drinking?*

Taylor and Hannah walk to their usual table in the cafeteria.

June's face lights up when she sees them. "I'm so excited about tonight. Hannah, you've got to come over and help me get ready. I'm gonna look so pretty." June glances over Hannah's shoulder. "Where's Eli?"

"Practising. He's really nervous about his audition tonight." Hannah takes a deep breath. "I can't help you get ready tonight. I'm going to Eli's audition. We might be able to make it after but —"

"He's not invited."

"What?"

"It's my first high school party. I can't have him there."

"Why not?"

"You know why."

"No, I don't."

"He's a loser."

"He's my friend."

"Is this about the Loser?" asks Max from the far end of the table.

"Hannah's not coming to the party tonight so she can hang out with him," whines June.

The colour drains from Max's cheeks. "Well, then … she's a … loser too."

"Shut up, Max," shoots June. She turns to Hannah. "You're really going to pick him over me?"

Everyone at the table stares at June and Hannah.

"I'm not picking him over you. I can pick both."

"But why would you want to?"

"I told you already. He's my friend too."

"I'm your best friend. And I have lots of friends." Hannah rolls her eyes. "So, if you want to stay my best friend, you'll be at my party tonight!"

Heat fills Hannah's chest. "And if I don't want to stay your best friend?"

June's mouth hangs open. "I … I…"

"I'm not coming to your stupid party, June!" Hannah storms away from the table. Her first instinct is to stomp to the band room, but she stops midstep.

Eli is practising for his audition tonight, she thinks. *I shouldn't bother him.*

Hannah turns and looks at June from across the room. Some of her anger melts away. Even from a distance June's makeup looks perfect. She looks like the most popular girl in the school. She's the girl who hangs out with Max after school and holds parties Eli isn't invited to. Parties with drinking. But behind the makeup, Hannah can see her childhood friend. The girl who used squeal excitedly every time Hannah walked into a room.

What happened to that June? she wonders.

Hannah sighs, turns away from the table, and leaves the cafeteria. With nowhere else to go, she walks to the gym. It's empty, and Hannah feels instantly calmer. She takes out her lunch and finishes her sandwich. She daydreams about playing on the court below.

17 STARTING TRYOUTS

Hannah stands under a hoop. It's the first day of tryouts. Around her, players warm up. At another basket, Taylor takes a powerful dribble toward the basket and scores a strong shot.

Everyone is so good, Hannah thinks.

As Hannah sets up for a form shot, she spots June entering the gym. She wonders how June's party went.

Hannah catches June's eyes. They hold a long stare. But neither girl moves toward the other.

The head coach strides into the gym and blows her whistle. Hannah jogs to centre court. "Welcome to the first day of grade nine basketball tryouts. I'm Coach Shannon. It's exciting to have so many players here. We're going to start with a layup drill. Everyone get in two lines."

Hannah jogs to the back of a line on one side of the court.

There are so many players. How am I supposed stand out? she wonders.

The drill begins. When Hannah gets to the front of the line, she catches the ball, takes two hard right-handed dribbles to the basket, and easily scores a right-handed layup. She jogs to the back of the rebounding line.

"I thought you were left-handed," says Taylor while they wait to get to the front of the rebounding line.

"I am."

"That layup looked so smooth."

Heat fill her cheeks. "Thanks." She watches the other players. Every single player scores their right-handed layup. The heat drains from her cheeks.

Coach Shannon blows the whistle. "We're going to do power layups. This may be new for —"

Suddenly, Hannah feels a tug on her shirt. She turns. June is suddenly behind her. "I want to talk."

Hannah's heart thumps in her chest. *How am I supposed to know how to do a power layup if June is talking to me?* Hannah keeps her eyes focused on Coach Shannon.

June tries again. "Hannah. Did you hear me?"

"I wasn't at basketball camp. I don't know how to do power layups," whispers Hannah. "I need to listen."

June's body stiffens.

"A power layup is the same as a regular layup except, at the end, you jump off two feet. That gives you more balance," Coach Shannon explains.

The drill begins. In front of Hannah, Taylor gets the ball. Hannah watches her take a strong dribble to the hoop. She steps with her left foot, then her right foot. Then she puts down both feet and jumps. Taylor scores her layup.

Left. Right. Jump, Hannah thinks.

Hannah catches the ball and does her best to do the footwork properly. The jump feels strange, but she manages to stay balanced and find the rim with her eyes. She shoots and scores.

By the end of the tryout, sweat drips from Hannah's forehead. Around her, several girls breathe heavily.

I'm so glad I've been playing with the boys every day, Hannah thinks.

"We're going to end tryouts with a scrimmage," announces Coach Shannon.

"Sweet," says Taylor under her breath.

"There are four teams. I've assigned each of you a team and a person on another team I want you to defend," Coach Shannon says. "Team A is Taylor, Manjeet, Hannah, Zoey, and Kaia. Team A will begin against Team B: June, Joelle, Mindy, Malaya, and Felicity. Hannah, you'll be checking June …"

Hannah gulps as the coach assigns the rest of the checks.

"The first team to three baskets gets to keep playing. All the other teams will wait on the sideline," finishes the coach.

Hannah walks onto the court and stands beside June. June stares at her coldly.

Taylor and Mindy stand in the centre circle. Coach Shannon throws the ball into the air. Taylor jumps and tips the ball toward June and Hannah. Hannah reaches out to grab the ball, but June bumps Hannah with her hip. June grabs the ball and passes it up the court to her teammate. June's team scores an easy basket.

Kaia brings the ball up the court and looks to Hannah's side of the court. June aggressively defends Hannah. Hannah takes one hard step toward the three-point line, plants her foot, and cuts hard to the basket. Kaia passes Hannah the ball. June is totally out of position. Taylor's defender steps in to stop Hannah. Hannah finds her balance, and passes the ball to Taylor, who scores.

"Nice pass," says Coach Shannon from the sideline.

Hannah sprints back on defence. Team B's point guard, Felicity, stares in June's direction. Hannah shifts her weight to the balls of her feet. As Felicity releases the ball, Hannah lunges forward. She tips the ball down the court. As Hannah moves to chase after the ball, June grabs at her wrist.

I want that ball! Hannah rips her wrist away from June's grip.

The whistle blows. "Foul!" announces Coach Shannon. "Team A's ball."

"Whatever," mutters June.

Manjeet takes the ball out of bounds. She passes it to Kaia, who waits patiently. Taylor sprints toward the basket and Kaia passes her the ball. Taylor scores!

Joelle takes the ball out of bounds. She carelessly tosses the ball in Felicity's direction. But before Felicity can catch it, Taylor swoops in front of her, steals the ball, and scores an easy layup.

"Three!" yells Taylor

"Team A wins," says Coach Shannon. "Team C. You're up!"

★★★

When tryouts are done, Hannah sits in the bleachers and takes off her shoes.

"Nice work today," says Taylor. "We won three in a row!"

"We did! You played great. You scored most of our points."

Taylor shrugs humbly. She looks over Hannah's shoulder. "Eli's here."

Hannah packs her belonging into her backpack and joins him.

"I made the orchestra!" announces Eli. He's grinning from ear to ear.

"Congrats!" Hannah hops up the stairs and without thinking gives Eli a big hug. At first, he freezes and goes stiff as a board. But after a moment, his body relaxes and he hugs Hannah back.

"Aww … Isn't that cute," says a voice from behind

them. Hannah looks up. It's Max. "First, you don't come to June's party. Now, you're hugging the Loser?"

Eli looks away from Max. But then he looks him directly in the eye. "Shut up, Max."

Max clenches his fists. Before he can reply, there's a loud sound thumping up the steps. It's June. She refuses to look at Hannah.

June stomps up to Max. "You're walking me home."

"I am?" asks Max.

"Yes. Let's go."

As they leave the gym, Max looks over his shoulder at Eli. Eli doesn't look away. Instead, he keeps staring Max right in the eye.

There's a moment of silence. Max turns and follows June out of the gym.

"So … you just stood up to Max," says Hannah, with a smile.

"I did, didn't I? It must be making the orchestra. It gave me superpowers or something."

"No superpowers. That was all you."

Eli blushes. There's another moment of comfortable silence.

"Is everything okay with you and June?" Eli says, looking sideways at Hannah.

"I was wondering when you were going to ask."

"I figured something was up. We've been eating in the hallway this week"

"I like it in the hallway better," admits Hannah. "I

think that's the weird part. I'm not mad ..." Hannah thinks about June grabbing her wrist on the court. "Or, I'm not *all* mad. I think I'm kind of sad, actually."

"What about?"

Hannah takes a deep breath and gets up. She knows the answer. She's been thinking a lot about her second goal. But it's different to say it out loud. Hannah and Eli walk out of the school in silence.

"I haven't talked to June since before the party," begins Hannah. Outside, her breath is visible in the dark November air. She can imagine her words being spelled out in front of her. "But I don't really miss her. I don't think that's how you're supposed to feel about your best friend."

There's a long silence.

"That's hard," says Eli finally.

"It is." Hannah shakes her head. "But I've got to stay focused on basketball."

"Okay," says Eli. "Why don't you tell me all about the tryout? Did you score lots of baskets?"

"A few," says Hannah with a smile.

18 THE LAST TRYOUT

Midway through the final tryout, Hannah sprints down the court. Her legs feel heavy, but she pushes herself to keep going. When Hannah gets to the three-point line, she makes a sharp turn toward the basket.

I have to make this layup or we're going to have to do the drill again, Hannah tells herself.

Kaia throws Hannah the ball. The pass is hard and fast. Hannah catches the ball and jumps toward the basket. She scores the layup.

Hannah breathes a sigh of relief.

"Thank you," says Kaia, coming over to give Hannah a high-five. "I don't think I could've done another round."

Hannah looks out onto the court. Other players are trying to complete the drill by scoring two layups in a row. "You got it, girls!" yells Hannah encouragingly.

The whistle blows. "Water break," announces Coach Shannon. "While you're getting water, I want you to get in these teams: June, Manjeet, Kaia, Zoey, and Hannah …"

Hannah looks over at June. They lock eyes. June's expression is blank.

I always used to know what June was thinking, thinks Hannah.

She looks around as the players gather into their teams. Taylor is standing beside Claudia, the best point guard in the gym. Hannah realizes that Taylor's team is stacked with skilled players.

Hannah looks at another team. Mindy passes Lauren the ball. But Lauren doesn't get her hands up in time, and it whacks her in the chest. Both girls laugh loudly.

Shouldn't one of them be on Taylor's team so the teams will be fair? Hannah wonders as she goes to stand with her own team.

"This is all right," says Manjeet, looking at her teammates.

"We're awesome," says June.

"No," corrects Manjeet. "That team is awesome." She points at Taylor's team.

"They've got all the best players," whines June.

"I want June's team and Malaya's team on the court," announces Coach Shannon.

The players walk onto the court. Hannah studies the players on Malaya's team: Elsa, Felicity, Sarah, and Joelle. Like Hannah's team, the players on Malaya's team are good, but not the best in the gym.

"Hannah, don't stare. It's weird," says June suddenly.

"That's the first thing you've said to me in days."

"You haven't been talking to me either."

Hannah looks around the gym, and then back at the players on the court. Suddenly, it clicks. "We're being tested. That team," explains Hannah, pointing at Mindy's team, "has all the worst players. Those are the players who aren't making the team."

June looks at Taylor's team. "And those are the players that are already on the team. And we're not on either of those teams."

"Right," says Hannah. Her stomach tightens.

"So, if we don't play well, we're going to be cut from the team."

"Right," says Hannah again. Her mouth is suddenly dry, and the sound comes out as a whisper. *All my work this year comes down to this game.*

"So, who does everyone want to guard?" asks Manjeet brightly.

Hannah looks at the other team. "I'll take Elsa."

The other players nod and sort out their checks. Hannah's heart is banging so loudly she can hear it in her ears.

Hannah closes her eyes. She remembers the feeling of standing on the outdoor basketball court. She can almost feel the wind against her skin while practising her layups. *I can do right-handed layups now.*

She remembers timing her drills. *I've gotten so much faster.*

She remembers playing with Luke and the boys.

This is just another basketball game. I've played lots of basketball games this year.

Hannah takes a deep breath. Coach Shannon throws the ball into the air. Manjeet jumps and taps it toward June. June catches the ball and passes to Hannah.

Hannah looks at the basket. Elsa is directly in front of her. *What am I going to do? I need to prove myself.*

Out of the corner of her eye, she sees June sprinting down the court.

June loves to cut, she remembers.

Hannah waits. Suddenly, June blasts past her defender and charges toward the basket. Hannah passes her the ball. June scores.

As June runs back on defence, she yells, "Nice pass!"

On defence, Hannah gets into position. Elsa is quick, so Hannah gives her a bit of space. Suddenly, Elsa runs toward June's check. She stops directly beside her, sets her feet, and crosses her arms over her chest.

"Screen coming!" yells Hannah, but it's too late. As June tries to defend her check, Malaya, she runs into Elsa. Malaya charges toward the basket and scores.

Zoey brings the ball up the court. She passes to Manjeet, who drives toward the basket and takes an off-balance shot. Hannah rushes toward the ball. Elsa is at Hannah's shoulder, but Hannah reaches out and yanks the ball away from Elsa's hands.

"Here!" yells June. She sprints to help Hannah with the rebound. It's strange, but Hannah knows exactly where June is going to stop. Hannah passes to that spot.

June makes a motion to Hannah with her head. Hannah knows June wants her to cut. Hannah cuts toward the basket, and June passes her the ball. Hannah scores an easy layup.

"Nice pass!" she yells as she runs back on defence.

After a few passes, Malaya has the ball again. Hannah sees Elsa move to go and screen. She looks at Malaya and Elsa. *They're about the same size,* Hannah thinks.

June reaches out and pokes the ball away from Malaya. It goes out of bounds.

Hannah jogs over to June. "When they screen, we need to switch checks."

"But we've never practised that," says June.

"We can do it," says Hannah.

"But what if we can't? I don't want to look stupid."

"Do you want to make the team?" Hannah and June lock eyes. "Come on, June."

"Fine. We'll try."

The other team passes the ball onto the court. Malaya receives the ball on the wing and Elsa runs to set a screen.

"Screen coming, June," warns Hannah under her breath. "We're going to switch."

Elsa sets her feet and puts her arms over her chest, getting ready to set a screen. Malaya dribbles toward them.

Hannah sees that June is in the wrong position.

She reaches out and grabs June, pulling her toward Elsa. Hannah pushes off her back foot and jumps out to meet Malaya. Startled by Hannah's presence, Malaya picks up the ball. She moves to pass it to a teammate. But as she throws the ball, Zoey darts in and tips it away. She sprints down the court with the ball and scores an easy layup.

Coach Shannon blows the whistle. "Hannah's team wins. They can stay on offence."

June runs over to Hannah. "We make a good team!" Her expression is bright and warm.

There's the old June, thinks Hannah. "We do," she says.

June gives Hannah a high-five.

Maybe we don't have to be best friends, thinks Hannah. *Maybe it's enough that we play well together.*

The next team walks onto the court. June looks at Hannah. They nod at each other and walk together to meet the other players.

The tryout continues with several more games. Hannah's team loses to Taylor's team the first time they meet. But in their third game, Hannah's team wins three to two.

When the game is over, the players shoot free throws in pairs. Hannah is paired with June. The girls don't chat as they shoot, but the silence isn't tense. Hannah didn't think she could have comfortable silences with June anymore.

When it's Hannah's turn, her hands are shaking with

nerves. She takes a breath, and focuses on her form.

Elbow, she reminds herself.

She shoots, and the ball falls through the mesh of the hoop.

"Nice shot," says June.

"Thanks."

Coach Shannon blows the whistle and the players gather around her. "It's been an excellent tryout, and I'm impressed with how hard everyone has worked. I'll post the team roster on the gym door by tomorrow at lunch."

19 TEAM SELECTION

Hannah sits in math class. Her knee bounces up and down madly. She taps her pencil against her book in time with her bouncing knee.

"Hannah?" says Jacob, the boy behind her.

"What?" she snaps.

"My desk is shaking," answers Jacob nervously.

"Oh … sorry."

She stops bouncing her knee, and looks down at her math worksheet. With the exception of a couple of doodles, it's empty.

How am I supposed to focus on Math when I'm about to get cut from the basketball team? she wonders.

Suddenly, the bell rings. Hannah looks at Eli with wide eyes. "I'm so nervous I feel sick. And I still have to make it through two more classes."

"You can do it. Meet me back here, and we'll walk to the gym together."

"Okay." Hannah nods.

For Hannah, the two classes between Math and

lunch are the longest classes in recorded history. When the lunch bell finally rings, she jumps up from her desk and speed walks to the math classroom.

"It's lunch. The list is up." Hannah says to Eli. She starts to breathe more quickly. "I don't know if I can do this."

"You can," says Eli. "Come on."

Hannah follows Eli down the hall. Her mouth is dry. There's a part of her that wants to sprint to the gym. There's another part that wants to run out of the school completely. Hannah sees the piece of paper stuck to the gym door with thick white masking tape.

Taylor is the first one to stride up to the door. She reads the list and nods. One of Taylor's friends gives Taylor a giant high-five.

Of course she made the team, Hannah thinks.

Hannah watches Manjeet walk up to the door. Manjeet stands completely still. Suddenly, she turns and hurries away from the door. There are tears in her eyes. She looks up at Hannah and then looks away quickly.

She must have got cut, guesses Hannah. *Manjeet's good. If she didn't make the team, what chance do I have?*

"You need to go look, Hannah," says Eli. "So you can read it yourself."

Hannah nods. It feels like her knees have turned into pudding. It's only eight steps, but her heart is pounding.

Hannah closes her eyes for a moment.

Please. Please. Please.

She opens her eyes and looks at the list: Taylor, Kate, Claudia, Ronda … Hannah.

Hannah blinks. She looks at the paper again. Her name is still there.

Suddenly, there is a squeal beside Hannah.

"I made it!" says June loudly. "So did you!" she adds.

"Yeah," says Hannah, in disbelief. "I made the team."

Hannah looks at June. June's expression is bright and familiar. She looks like Hannah's old friend.

June launches into Hannah's arms to give a hug. But Hannah doesn't get her arms up in time. The hug becomes more like a tackle. June releases Hannah and takes a step back. She looks to the ground, embarrassed. "I mean, it's cool that we're going to be teammates."

Hannah thinks about her second goal. "Totally."

"About last week … I shouldn't have made you choose between my party and Eli."

"Thanks. I shouldn't have yelled at you."

"So, we're okay?"

Hannah nods. "Yeah."

"But not the same," says June, half statement, half question.

Hanna takes a deep breath. "We haven't been the same for a while, I think." Hannah looks June in the eye. Her expression is soft. "And maybe that's okay."

For once, June is quiet. "Yeah … maybe it is. I'm going to go eat lunch. Do you want to come?" June pauses for a moment. She looks at Eli standing in the corner and then back at Hannah. "Eli could come too," she offers.

Hannah smiles and looks over her shoulder. Eli's stare is intense and inquisitive.

I haven't told him I made the team yet!

"Thanks for the invite, but I think I'm going to skip out today."

"Oh, okay."

"Tomorrow, though," says Hannah reassuringly.

"That'd be good," says June with a nod. "I'll see you at practice tonight?"

"Totally," confirms Hannah.

June walks away from the gym. The moment she's gone, Hannah speed walks to Eli.

"I made the team!"

"Congrats!" says Eli.

Hannah can't help herself. She leans over and gives him a big hug. She even lifts him off the floor slightly. When Hannah leans back, she's surprised to see that Eli's face isn't the least bit red. He's still smiling at Hannah proudly.

"I can't believe it."

"I can," says Eli. "You worked really hard this year."

"I did," says Hannah. She turns to Eli. "And I would never have been able to do it without you. Thank you."

"You're welcome," says Eli. "But you did all the hard stuff."

"I'm so excited," admits Hannah. She leads them

away from the gym.

"Where are we going?" asks Eli.

"To eat lunch and talk about orchestra."

"Really?"

"You had your first rehearsal this morning, didn't you?"

"I did!"

"I want to hear all about it."

As they leave the gym behind, Hannah feels a surge of pride. *All my work paid off! And tonight, I get to go to basketball practice with my team!*